# EVACUATION

## VACCINATION NOVEL BOOK 2

### PHILLIP TOMASSO

# Praise for VACCINATION

"I loved this book because of the concept; zombies didn't just appear after somebody woke up in a hospital bed! The group of survivors were believable, and I loved the fact that they weren't perfect. Highly recommended." – D.A. Wearmouth, bestselling author of *First Activation*

"VACCINATION is a thrill a minute. Narrated in a gritty noir voice, Phillip Tomasso drags you into a zombie outbreak face first and doesn't let you go until you've ripped your fingernails off clawing for help. Smart, intense and damn right frightening, VACCINATION is a must for any zombie fan."– Max Booth III, author of *Toxicity*

"It's hard not to get emotionally attached to the small group of survivors and root for them despite their personal flaws. It's pretty much impossible to describe the end without giving away too much. I'll just say that it was a great twist. Whether you are new to zombie fiction or have been a fan for years, I'd tell you to check this one out. It's a great read." – Ian McLellan, Zombie-Guide.com

"Tomasso created a Zombie book that seems all too possible! This book kept me wired tight from the beginning until the very end. If you like awesome adventure, and vivid storytelling, then you will LOVE *Vaccination*! 5 BIG Stars!" – Cedric Nye, author of *The Road to Hell is Paved with Zombies*

"There's a bit of a cliff hanger at the end of the book, which left me wanting more. I'm anxiously awaiting the publication of the second book. If you're looking for a great zombie book, then I highly recommend you grab a copy of Vaccination. Props to Phillip Tomasso for writing this fantastic zombie novel!" – J. Cornnell Michels, author of *Jordan's Brains*

"Tomasso explores a humanity left dormant in the infected with graceful elegance. While we get glimpses into that unexpected possibility throughout the book, I would have loved digging deeper down that rabbit hole and see what he would have gifted us with. Simply put, however, VACCINATION is on fire!" — The Bookie Monster

# Praise for Phillip Tomasso

"This is different ... confident, addictive storytelling, great characters, and an intriguing plot. You'll read it fast but remember it for a long time. " —Lee Child, best-selling author of *One Shot* and the *Jack Reacher* series

"(Tomasso) takes the standard fare of the private investigator genre and adds twists and turns to make it anything but standard. Tomasso's writing is crisp and clear ... thoroughly enjoyable." —Joseph Nassise, author of *Internal Games* and *King of the Dead*

*"Phillip Tomasso understands what drives people who live on the edge. His characters are three-dimensional and they engage your sympathy and your anger. . ."*— William Meikle, author of *Night of the Wendigo* and *The Midnight Eye Files*

*"I have a selection of authors that I turn to when I need a break from Fantasy and Phillip Tomasso has just become one of them."* —*The Eternal Night Magazine*

*"Phillip Tomasso breathes new life into an old genre – an EXCELLENT read!"* —M. R. Sellers, Author of *In the Bleak Midwinter* and *Never Burn a Witch*

Dedication

This book is for my son, Phil. He has been my sounding board, and biggest supporter. Without his help, I don't think the second book in the trilogy could have been completed! Thank you, buddy!

## Special Thanks

I need to thank my beta readers: Phillip Tomasso IV, Wendy LaForce, Sues Melia and Janice McFadden Mickolas. Also a huge thank you to Joe M. Diebold. He saved this story in a way most people could not. And to my family and friends at 911 for making VACCINATION such a success! You were the characters. I was just the scribe.

# PROLOGUE

Things spun out of control. Felt like months ago, instead of days, when life was . . . well, I wouldn't call it normal. You will never catch me calling it that. I worked four to midnight at 911, dispatching fire trucks, ambulances, and taking emergency calls. Tough job. I was trained to take a call, send help, and move on to the next. No looking back. It was easier said than done. Which was what I did, and made a living at it. The divorce had been the hard part. It kept me from moving forward and drained me of emotions. I wouldn't say I didn't give a fuck about anything, but I'd be hard pressed to put together a list.

One saving grace, which was a term I absolutely hated, were my kids, so the term was accurate. I had two. Charlene, who was a teenager and, unfortunately, becoming quite the beautiful young adult quickly; and Cash, who was nine and quiet and looked a lot like me.

Signs were there in the days before what I now thought of as Armageddon, melodramatic, I know, but again it felt accurate so I used it. I saw them *now*, but I hadn't realized what it all meant at the time. Don't think any of us did. It was the simple things. At work, people called off shifts--meaning they were supposedly too sick to come in. Or didn't call in at all and just didn't show up.

Calls that came in at work were strange, but honestly, no stranger than most summer nights. Fighting, biting, stabbings, shootings, toothaches, and infant deliveries. Nothing out of the ordinary. What could have been a red flag were the increased missing person calls. Loved ones who never made it home from work, school, from grocery shopping, or nights out on the town. Again, standard. Just the increased volume was odd for October.

I don't think the vaccination hit everyone at once. Didn't turn them all into zombies on the same night. It was a gradual escalation that finally said fuck it and went haywire. The reports on the news started the panic. Some homeless guy on a freeway eating the face off some other guy or people in college partaking in cannibalism. Hospital security calling to say dead bodies were missing from the morgue.

The clues were there. The signs. The red flags. Shouldn't need a group of kids in a Mystery Van with a dog connecting the dots. Yet, no one had done that. No one thought zombies. I mean, why would you?

You wouldn't. In fact, if someone had, we would label them a 78 and send a cop to check on their welfare, and stage an ambulance ready to transport the patient to a psychiatric wing at one of our many treating facilities.

*Me?* My divorce had been far from amicable. I didn't kill her or her boyfriend at *that* time. Thought about it. Now, don't get me wrong, I wanted to, but what would have been the point? She didn't want to be with me. Maybe I didn't make enough money? Wasn't a good enough husband? Didn't pay enough attention to her because I was busy working my ass off; crazy hours, trying to pay bills and put food on the table. I wasn't going to fight to keep someone who thought they needed a guy richer than me. Fuck that. Moreover, killing them would only land me in prison. Not that I would have cared. I think there would have been satisfaction in that. Rotting away in a cell, knowing, you didn't make an ass of me. Just yourself, baby.

Couldn't do it, though; I had two important reasons.

Charlene and Cash.

Bam! Right there it was. Cards on the table. I needed *not* to kill anyone so I could continue being a father to my children.

They were, and always have been, my priority. My first and only priority.

Once it became crystal clear that a fucking Armageddon had hit our planet, I had only one goal. Get my kids.

Wasn't a chance in hell I was going to leave them with my ex. She might be a good mother--I never indicated anything otherwise, but in times like these, times where zombies are eating people like starving kids with Happy Meals, no, they needed their father. I knew I'd be able to protect them. I knew I'd protect them better than she or her aged husband ever could.

Add the fact that I knew both she and her husband had been vaccinated against swine flu, and my time-is-of-the-essence mode kicked into high fucking gear. Let me tell you, high fucking gear.

I had met my goal. It hadn't been easy. Allison, my girlfriend and also a dispatcher from 911, and I had saved my kids. Charlene might only have been fourteen, but she'd taken care of Cash until we had reunited.

Then the military saved us; Border Patrol copter spotted us; Army rode in on a Humvee and got us off the plaza roof and into the vehicle.

Maybe that was why the worst thing I did was think; *now we're all safe, the nightmare has ended.*

I didn't *really* believe that. Might have thought it, but proof otherwise surrounded me.

We were packed tightly inside the Humvee. Two soldiers sat in front, with a gunner up top. My kids, scared to death, hugged me tight as shit. Allison looked as if she might start crying any second. Dave, well, he seemed all right. Back when Allison and I first met Dave and his brother on the way to rescue my kids, I thought he would be a hindrance, especially after his brother Josh was shot and killed. Dave kept an arm draped around that woman we'd saved outside the hotel, just prior to seeing the Border Patrol choppers--who in turn called the military out to help us. That woman was Sues Melia.

Sues, on the other hand, didn't look good. Her body trembled. I was just too tired to react other than to tell Dave.

"Hold her tighter, man. I think she might be going into shock."

"I got her," Dave said. He made me feel claustrophobic. Built like an ox, the other five of us barely had room to turn our heads. He looked as if he didn't have room to breathe.

A handful of days changed not just my entire life, but as best I could tell, the world's. At the very least, our country's. Here we were in Rochester, a previously dying city, sandwiched between two larger cities also in the midst of decay, and then in a blink, swine flu destroyed civilization.

Not the flu so much as the vaccination against it.

"Sir," I said. The soldiers made it clear they weren't answering questions. They didn't even seem to want us talking. They were kids, really. In their twenties. It didn't deter me, since I was at a point where I simply didn't give a fuck anymore. "We were just on I-390 north, and now we're on the parkway, east. Only thing I can think of is the Coast Guard station along the river. Is that where we're headed?" Border Patrol was right in the same general area. It had to be one of the two, best I could guess.

"I am not going to tell you again," the soldier in the passenger seat said. "Where we are going is classified."

"You know what? We're all in this together. Are you afraid I might share your precious intel with zombies? Give them a map with passwords and launch codes? You don't have to be a dick, Private."

Allison shot me a look. Felt it. Piercing blue eyes did just that. *Pierced.* I tried to shake off the intensity of the glare.

"Sir, your friend back there insisted we save you from the roof. We did. That's after the helicopter spotted you, and sent us to save you from the field. I recognize we're on the same side of the outbreak. Our mission, whether you like it or not, is to evacuate non-infected humans and to keep classified information, get this, classified. And I am not a Private, sir. I'm a Corporal."

Evidently, I got under his skin with a simple insult to rank, because he came unraveled. We were all on edge, but his weakness was apparent, too easy to spot. That couldn't be good. He was just scared. No different from anyone else. Didn't necessarily make him a dick, but I at least had his number. That was good enough, for now.

I remember having heard all kinds of facts about the flu; the respiratory disease introduced to humans from pigs. Can you beat that? I think the first case of the swine flu showing up in humans was verified, out of all places, in Mexico in 2009.

Like any virus, washing hands and covering your face when you sneezed or coughed might have prevented the epidemic. You know what, though? People are gross. Filthy. No different from pigs infecting us, really. We are the epitome of Orwell's *Animal Farm*. Just at a zombie-level. Wasn't going to be long before our race stepped aside and let the next semi-intelligent organism have a shot at running things. That, unfortunately, I believed.

It was in the autumn of '09 when a vaccination was made readily available to the public, and this is what bothers me most. I didn't have a heck of a lot of time to think this over the last several days. Here, now, sitting in the Humvee headed northeast, I did.

The call I'd taken the night all hell broke loose, pardon the cliché, is what got to me. The guy worked at some lab at one of the hospital campuses. He indicated that shipments of contaminated vaccination vials were shipped all over the U.S.

The contaminated vials still might have prevented people from getting the swine flu, but the side effects were more than bargained for. Anyone inoculated became a zombie.

My kids, Allison, Dave, Sues, I'm guessing, and these soldiers, must not have received the vaccinated shots. Therefore, we were not zombies.

The problem, and I am making this percentage up, is that like 80% of the country *did* receive their vaccination, were infected, and now spent their days trying to eat non-infected people. Unless it was raining. They hated rain, which would make Seattle residents generally safe in a *holy fuck it finally pays off for all of the terrible weather* kind of way.

The two things that seemed relevant--head shots killed zombies best, just like in all the b-horror films, and getting bitten, or scratched didn't seem to turn *non*-infected humans into flesh eating monsters. At least, so far as I could tell that just wasn't what happened.

So, again, what bothered me the most, I mean really nagged at me, and was the reason why I've never received the vaccination, ever? Here it is, kind of laid out in a nutshell:

How did the United States identify the cause of the flu in Mexico, develop a viable vaccination, and proceed to distribute it across our country in less than a year?

Science didn't work that way. Government sure as fuck didn't seem too, unless it served their best interest. Did that seem even remotely possible? Do we have a vaccine for the cold? A cure for headaches? I won't even touch on cancers and MS.

The answer is no, we don't. Yet, in months, we had a vaccination against the first outbreak of swine flu that, best I can remember, infected *one* Mexican?

We were close to Lake Ontario, worse, the Genesee River-- so excuse me if I smelled something fishy. I think *we* were involved in the disease, the spreading of it, possibly its creation and it just happened to come back and bite the US in the ass is all, literally. In the ass.

Does that make me a conspiracy theorist? Or an asshole? *Me?*

I didn't trust the fucking government at all. This was their mistake. I felt it and I knew it. Now, we're all just collateral damage. Collateral. Fucking. Damage.

# CHAPTER ONE

*Halloween, Saturday, 0958 hours*

Headed eastbound on the Lake Ontario State Parkway, we'd just passed the Latta Road exit when the Humvee came to a stop. Moments later, rapid machine gunfire erupted.

"We're not getting through," the driver said. I heard what sounded like a gloved fist pound a steering wheel. I would have asked, but it wasn't relevant.

"Make a path." Didn't need to see the Corporal to know he'd just checked the clip on his AK rifle, and smacked it back into place.

I missed my shovel. I don't remember what happened to it, where I had left it. Or my hockey stick. I'd done some damage in the mall with that thing. Slap shot.

I opened my mouth. Allison set a hand on my shoulder, which was clearly a passive way to shut me up, no doubt. I allowed it for the time being.

The engine revved and the Humvee lurched forward. We went up and over things, with the bumps making us bounce inside. I don't think the thing had shocks. The monster could climb over cars and boulders, but the engine protested with a long steady and loud whine.

"This isn't going to work," the driver said.

I sat facing the rear, staring at Dave and Sues. Dave's eyes were wide, watching whatever unfolded out the front windshield. There was not enough room for me to turn and look, not with kids on my knees and Allison beside me. "What's going on?"

"Can't tell," Dave said.

Out the side window, I saw zombies along the side of the road. They looked interested as they made their way toward us. The running ones were gunned down. The slow walking ones, ignored. The sound of the engine and the gunfire was what drew them at us in the first place. It was a Catch-22 if I had ever seen one.

"Must be obstacles in front of us," Dave said. "Cars maybe."

Cars, yes. Zombies, too, I'd bet. It felt like that might be what we crawled over, bodies, because I didn't hear metal crumble and glass pop and shatter.

I heard the driver yell, "I'm not leaving the vehicle. We'll get by this, through this, and be on our way."

"I see it," Dave said. "Couple of those eighteen wheelers, jack-knifed."

"They're not supposed to use this road," I said.

"Well, okay, but that's what's out there. Two of them. At least. That's about all I can see. One's on its side." Dave kept moving his head forward, back, side to side, as if it helped him see more out of the small front windshield or something. "And a ton of zombies. I mean, ton."

I pursed my lips. The kids didn't need to hear that. I could have kicked Dave in the shin. He deserved it, too. "They'll get us through," I said. I wanted to sound confident, the way a parent should. Comforting and confident.

Trouble was, I knew I didn't because I wasn't.

Cash cried. Not sobbed. His body didn't shake. Tears just slid down his cheeks.

"We're safe in here," I said. "They are the military. They're trained for this. They have guns and are skilled at using them.

We're going to get past this roadblock. They're taking us somewhere safer, and far away from here."

"Sit tight, everyone," the Corporal said. He opened his door, hopped out of the Humvee. The driver did, too. I heard the hood pop open.

I had spoken far too soon, and freely. I looked like a liar. Can't tell kids we're getting out of here and a second later the driver gets out of the Humvee and pops the hood. It just detracts from the validity of every fucking thing you just said.

"The engine?" Allison said.

Dave nodded. "Looks like it."

This wasn't good. Couldn't be. That engine hadn't been screaming for attention long. No way could it give out so quickly. These things were built for battle, all terrain. Cruising over bodies shouldn't have touched the mechanics of such a beast.

I don't know how long we sat where we were with no one saying a word. We just stared at one another, waiting. I don't think I thought about anything. I just stared, at Dave, Sues, my kids, and when I turned my head to the right, at Allison.

When the side door opened, the Corporal stood there. "We're moving on foot. Let's go."

"Where are we headed? Don't tell me it's classified. Something happens to you, or your buddies, we need to know where to go. You owe us that," I said.

"You called it. Coast Guard. Other side of the O'Rourke Bridge, over the Genesee, then down by the pier," he said without an argument. He wore sunglasses, so I couldn't see his eyes, but I felt them, felt fear radiate from his entire facial expression.

I knew right where the Coast Guard station was; not because I was, or had been, a dispatcher for 9-1-1, but because I took my kids fishing in the area. Often. Filled a cooler with juice pouches, and sandwiches and chips. With those collapsible chairs, and coffees for the three of us, yes, all three of us, we'd head out early morning and fish off the edge into the river. Spend hours there. Catch a lot of perch and sunfish and carp, give them a kiss and throw them back in. They loved it. I loved it.

"Okay," I said to everyone inside. "Let's go. We stay close, together. Got it? Charlene, don't let go of my hand." I wasn't putting Cash down. He was going up on my back, or in my arms, but not down.

We climbed out of the Humvee with the Corporal's assistance.

We stood in front of the vehicle. The driver was on my left, the Corporal on my right, and the soldier that had manned the gun on top, took point.

I removed my backpack, which I had filled with supplies earlier at my apartment. Canned food, and clothing. A phone charger for Charlene's cell. I wasn't going to be able to keep it on my back. I swapped it out for my son. He sat up high, arms around my shoulders.

I read the name sewn on the man's shirt: CORPORAL SPENCER.

"What's in the bag?" Spencer said.

"Food. Clothes."

"You don't need it. We have supplies. Plenty."

I didn't just want to leave it. I removed the charger, stuffed it in my pocket. I tossed the bag against the Humvee. "You're sure?"

"Positive, sir."

"And what about us?" I said.

"Sir?"

"Guns. Give us your side arms. Something. You can't--"

"You are *not* getting guns."

"I never fired a gun," Sues said. She wasn't helping the argument. Hurt it, actually.

"Dave and I, we can shoot well." It was partly a lie. I had no clue if Dave had ever seen a gun before. "You've got to give us something."

"Can't do that, sir. Stay inside the circle," Spencer said.

They barked orders. Their weapons kept us covered. We moved from disabled vehicle to disabled vehicle. The soldiers checked inside each one. I don't think they looked for keys. More than likely it was for zombies. Don't want to hide with your back to a car that has more danger inside than what you faced outside.

Felt like square one to me. We stopped by the roof of a cargo van on its side. Two of the military guys peeked around an end, checking to see if the coast was clear.

"Why don't you radio in for backup, for more help," Dave said. His voice boomed with authority. He stood with one arm protectively wrapped around Sues' shoulder. "I mean--if we're just going across the bridge, help's not far. Call them. Why don't you just radio them?"

"We have, sir. We're the first patrol this close to returning. The other two are still miles away," Corporal Spencer said. His green fatigues did nothing to blend in with abandoned vehicles on a street.

"So there's what? Three teams? Three?" I said.

Spencer looked at me. I hated the sunglasses now. "We need to move."

"How many Border Patrol? Just the two in the helicopter? We talking about a rescue party of like what, eleven or twelve people?" I said. "Is that it?"

"Sir, we're not staying here. We are meeting at the Coast Guard facility and moving out from there."

"To where?"

"Right now, sir, I don't see how that matters much. If we don't get our asses across that bridge, more of those things will come out of the woods for us. Don't know if you've seen the fast ones, but if they come at us, most of us are as good as dead. Do you understand? Do you?"

I nodded. Spencer showed some balls and I respected that. "Give me your sidearm."

"We're not doing that," the driver of the Humvee said.

"Do it," Spencer said.

"Sir?"

Spencer pulled a 9mm from his hip holster and handed it to me. The driver reluctantly handed his pistol over to Dave.

"Pettenski, you too," Spencer said.

Pettenski, who'd operated the machine gun, held his handgun out between Allison and Sues. Sues just stared at it, made no move. Allison swiped it up, checked the clip and nodded at me.

"Spade, anything moves on the right, shoot first. We're out of time for questions. Pettenski, let's roll."

Let's roll? Did military people really say that?

Didn't matter. What did matter was that we had weapons, instead of gardening tools. While it might only be three guys, it was a military escort. Men trained for combat. I had no problem with that.

What I had a problem with was the pack of zombies that just crossed the bridge, and was moving westbound right toward *us*.

# CHAPTER TWO

The van we hid behind would work until the group was on us. After that, we'd be vulnerable.

"Should we hide?" Sues said. She turned her head, spun her body to follow. She did a full three-sixty. "There must be someplace to hide."

"Spade, how many do you count?" Spencer said.

"The way they were moving, they're the slow ones, sir. Best I can tell, anyway. Must be between twenty-five and thirty. Hard to get a good count. Could be more behind them that just aren't visible at this angle with the sun where it is."

Spencer nodded and then he did the oddest thing. He looked at me. "Thoughts?"

Must be because I appeared to be the leader of my own squad. Or because Spencer was probably twenty years old and I reminded him of his fucking dad or something. "Have a lot of extra clips for these guns?" I said.

The zombies were already across the bridge and crossing Lake Avenue. They were making their way down the parkway now. Why they hadn't gone left or right, or split up, I had no idea. Point was; they hadn't. They continued to make their way west.

Spencer patted at the gear on him. I didn't see anything other than the Kevlar vest, a flashlight, cuffs and mace. Must have been more items inside the various pockets. I trusted he knew what he was talking about. "Way I figure, the tipped van is as good a place as any to make a stand. We put the kids inside. Those things won't be returning fire, so it's not like there's danger from a gas tank getting hit. With six of us, we should be able to clear them."

"Only downfall is that the shots will attract more," Pettenski said. "They'll come from everywhere. Out of the woodwork, you know?"

"We'd have to do it quick. Like shooting gallery style," Spencer said. "Are you a good shot?"

"I won't miss," I said. It was as true a statement as any. The herd was massive and appeared to be growing, spreading. I just had to fire into it. If I missed a target that size, shame on me.

Dave just kept nodding up and down. "I like it, Chase. I do. I like it."

I looked at Allison. Her eyes were easy to read. She was in. "Kids, I'm going to put you into the van. Fast," I said, because once I got onto the vehicle and slid open the cargo door, we'd have been spotted. Cover blown.

"I'm fighting," Charlene said. I expected it.

"Not this time. You're going to protect your brother. That's what I need you to do. No arguments. Not now. You want to be mad, fine. You want to discuss it, fine. But after. Understand?" I said. I wasn't yelling. I definitely grit my teeth while I spoke though. I needed my daughter to understand that this was not me being mad, but I was serious and there was no time for compromise. She got it.

"Take my hand, Cash," she said.

"On three, I'm going to jump up onto the side of the van and slide the door open," I said.

"We'll hand the kids up."

"I'm not a kid," Charlene said.

I shot her a look.

She lowered her eyes.

14

Silently, I counted out three, showing my fingers.

Dave quickly laced his hands together. I stepped into the makeshift stand. He hoisted me up and I scrambled to slide the door open.

"Sir," I heard Pettenski say. I was tempted to look around.

Staying as focused as one can in such a situation, I tugged on the door handle. It did not budge. I kneeled on the sliding door, tried the passenger door, and it lifted open. "The kids," I said.

"Sir," Pettenski said, again.

The military opened fire. The sound of their rifle shots was not as loud as I'd expected. On the other hand, maybe my head was so filled with rushing blood that my hearing was impacted.

Cash was handed to me first. He stayed low, belly flat on the fiberglass. I helped him drop into the van. "Come on, Charlene," I said.

Dave practically tossed her up. She inserted herself through the open door. "Stay low, and safe," I said.

Only now did I allow myself to look, after I closed the passenger door. I wished I'd remained blissfully blind to what came at us.

The zombies might have appeared sluggish crossing the bridge, but a good chunk of them was fast, though. Half, maybe. Judging from the amount of gunfire I heard, to the few zombies that actually went down, they were also harder to hit. Way harder to kill.

And my kids were now locked inside a tipped-on-its-side van. Locked. Better than the thought of trapped. If this went bad, though, trapped is what they'd become.

I stayed on one knee on the side of the van and aimed. I fired off two shots.

Below was chaos. The military guys yelled back and forth. Too much yelling, if you ask me. They made everything more confusing. I couldn't listen to what was said, or shouted, because I needed to concentrate. I wanted every bullet to hit true. The distraction made it a hundred times more complicated.

At least ten of the fast zombies were almost on us. I couldn't take the time to count. I had no idea how many bullets this clip held. Seven? Ten? No clue.

I think I missed my first two. The next three, I hit the target, but not on the bull's eye. A shoulder, gut and heart shot. Any other time, that might be considered all right. With zombies, it had to be a head shot. Kill the brain. Destroy it.

That's when I noticed the other vehicle on its side. I mean, I'd seen it. Just hadn't thought of using it. I closed one eye, aiming for the gas tank and let off two quick shots.

I worried I'd seen too many movies.

Thought for sure I was out of my mind after squeezing the trigger, but something sparked, and the car exploded. A giant black mushroom cap, raised into the air by a pillar of flames, erupted. Most of the fast zombies still ran at us, but as human torches.

Black smoke billowed up from their outstretched arms.

Slowly they fell, crawled at us, and then stopped.

Someone yelled something about nice shooting.

It had been. Have to pat myself on the back after. The explosion took out plenty of zombies, but there were more. Many more.

"We're being flanked," I heard. Thought it might be Spade.

Flanked. Did that mean more zombies from a different direction?

"I'm out," I said, and turned. "I need more ammo!"

Spencer tossed over a clip.

I almost missed it. It bounced on my fingers and I wrapped them around and as quickly as I could, and reloaded.

"We need to move forward. Charge the remaining zombies," Pettenski said.

I fired and landed a headshot, then another.

The fast zombies seemed neutralized. Dead. Really dead. The slow ones had not stopped though. They continued toward us. They dragged limbs with labored steps. Sounded ironic, but they did not look well.

Hungry? Would starvation kill them eventually? Could starvation kill something that was already supposedly dead?

"Chase, get your kids," Spencer said.

I didn't like it. The idea of moving made me apprehensive. Sweat dripped from my forehead into my eyes. I ignored the sting and pulled open the van door. Charlene sat on the glass by the driver's side with Cash cradled in her lap. "We're moving. Let's go," I said, as my arm lunged into the van.

Cash grabbed on. I pulled him out and set him next to me.

His silence was almost too much. He cried, but did not otherwise make a sound. I hated to think about the trauma he felt. I did not forget that he'd just lost his mother and that alone had to affect his mind.

Charlene refused my hand. She climbed up and out on her own. She was traumatized, too. She was hell-bent on showing me that she was independent, and capable of fighting side-by-side, and that she no longer wished to be treated like a child. She'd proved it several times since the outbreak, but I was her father. We didn't let go of our little girls. Not easily. Not while there was still fight left in us. At least, that was the way I saw it. I wished she didn't work so hard to show me how traumatized she *wasn't*.

We scrambled down off the van. I did not want to run, because it seemed more dangerous. We'd be fully exposed. Shooting had been a challenge as it was, running and shooting sounded impossible.

Pettenski, Spade and Spencer had their knees bent, rifles raised. They encircled us.

I knelt down. "Climb up, sport," I said.

Cash grabbed onto my neck. He was nine but weighed a ton. Or at least sixty pounds. It felt like a ton, but it didn't matter, I'd carry him. Couldn't have him trying to run and keep up. I wasn't going to lose him or Charlene. They were all that mattered, more now than ever.

"Stay close," I said. Charlene nodded. The attitude was gone. For now, anyway.

# CHAPTER THREE

To say the situation looked hopeless sounded nothing short of melodramatic to an extent. It appeared that way, though. Hopeless. Zombies came at us from nearly every direction. The sound of gunfire attracted them like flies to shit.

Spade took point, working to lead us closer to the bridge. The boy could shoot. No doubt about it. He'd let one rip. Headshot. Pivot one way, headshot. Pivot the other, headshot. If it weren't such a dire situation, I would have applauded.

Instead, I stayed low and followed. I shifted Cash around on my back, trying to hold him with my arms. It was an awkward angle, mainly because my gun was tucked into the front waistband of my pants. He had his arms wrapped tightly around my shoulders. I felt his breath, quick, shallow and hot on my neck. "How are you doing, buddy?"

"I'm okay, Dad."

Behind me was Charlene, and behind her, Allison. Dave and Sues stood beside me. Spencer took up the rear, and right side. Pettenski had the rear and left covered.

The idea wasn't much different from when pioneers crossed the new frontier. When natives attacked, the wagon trains ran in a tight circle. It was an attempt to create a kind of moving and fortified structure. I never studied the era, and westerns were never my style, so I had no idea how it turned out for them. Skilled Native Americans launching arrows at covered wagons. Seemed like the guys at the reins were sitting targets. Literally.

Right now, with three military guys around us, I didn't feel that safe, or secure.

We weren't out of bullets, but I couldn't help worry there were more zombies than ammo. Hand-to-hand combat seemed like a terrible idea. I was ahead of myself, I know. We weren't there, yet. Not yet that far gone.

"Keep moving, keep moving," Spencer said. "Don't stop."

I don't know who he thought had stopped and looked back, because our group was walking. Everyone pushed forward. Spencer might just be barking out orders for the sake of yelling. We didn't need the added tension.

Spade ejected a clip, dropped it, slapped in a new one and went right back to firing off shot after shot without missing a single beat, or skull. We continually had to step over and walk around the wake of proof. If there was still a government in place at the end of all of this, I planned to nominate the guy for whatever awards were available.

"Dad," Cash said.

"Yeah, buddy? What?" I said. Now was not the best time to talk.

"They're getting closer," he said.

"We're okay," Charlene said. She spoke to her brother the way her mother might have--her voice calm, soothing. I knew she was just as scared as Cash, and as I was. Her insides had to be as shaky as mine felt. I didn't catch a trace of any of that in her tone of voice.

"We just keep walking, Cash. We stay close. We keep walking," I said. I smelled something burning. Nearby something had to be on fire. The sky was blue. I did not see any pillars of black smoke rising. There was no mistaking the combined odor of old clapboard, wires, carpeting, clothing, upholstery and flesh.

Cash had been right, though. As good a shot as Spade was, as much as we were able to keep moving forward, there seemed an endless stream of monsters converging. Simply an endless wave of them.

It felt hard not to run. Running seemed more natural. If we ran, there would be no way to stay in a tight group; no way for the encircling protection to work as well as it had been. Fighting the urge to sprint took willpower.

"Something's on fire," Dave said.

"I smell that," Sues said. "I can't tell where it's coming from."

"It's behind us," Spencer said. "A house or something. Forget about it. We're going the opposite way. Keep moving."

"I'm out," Spade said. "Out."

My heart and stomach swapped spots. I think my knees wobbled some. "Now what?"

"Me, too," Pettenski said.

Spencer nodded. "We're going to run. Launch grenades there, and there. And there."

Spencer pointed to the front, left and right. At angles.

Spade threw the first grenade. It landed toward Lake Avenue, at the largest group of gathered zombies. Limbs flew when it exploded.

There was little time to take in the horror. We were running. I kept my arms behind me, holding onto Cash. Charlene and Allison were on either side.

More grenades detonated around us, the soldiers pulled pins and tossed more and more as we ran. It was an effective way to take out large numbers of zombies at once. But not all of them. Not nearly enough of them,

Over all, it did seem to be working. "Dave," I said.

"We're right behind you," he said.

That was what I wanted to hear. We came to the Lake Avenue intersection. The O'Rourke Bridge was dead ahead.

"Fast zombies, sir," Spade said. "I've got one left."

"Pettenski?" Spencer said.

"One."

We ran. They talked. Spencer used his radio. "Sergeant Vitale? Sergeant? This is Corporal Spencer."

I just noticed the pod in his ear. I wasn't going to be able to hear the second half of the conversation. I did not know where Spade spotted the zombies. Must be behind us, but I couldn't look back, because I would trip. Cash and I would go down. I needed to pay attention to my footing--on reaching our destination.

The one thing that looked a little promising was that the bridge finally appeared clear.

"Throw them," Spencer said.

I did not see where the last two grenades were launched, but I heard them explode. It was behind us.

"We're out," Spade said.

I ran as fast, and as hard as I could. Felt the burning in my lungs. Muscles around my stomach tightened. Squeezed. I wouldn't be able to keep it up. Adrenaline only lasted so long. We'd been at it awhile, and I felt drained.

"Keep running, Daddy," Cash said. I wondered if he heard my thoughts, or read my mind.

"We're not stopping, not until we're somewhere safe."

Spencer said, "Pettenski! Pettenski, get back here!"

"Sir," Spade said.

"No, we keep running."

I had to look. I did not like being blind.

Pettenski had stopped on the bridge. He held a long knife in each hand. He was going to take them on alone. With knives.

"I can't let him do this alone," Spade said.

"We have orders. We need to get the civilians to the Coast Guard. You know that, Private First Class! Pettenski is buying us time to complete this mission. You will stay with us!" Spencer sounded as winded as I felt.

No one ran very fast right now. Pettenski earned all of our attention. You might call him crazy, a rebel, but to me, Pettenski was a hero. A martyr.

The first fast zombie reached Pettenski. He dropped down, swept its leg, and drove his blade into the back of its neck once it landed face down on the asphalt. Like a coiled spring,

Pettenski shot back up to his feet in time to grab the arm of a second zombie. He drove the blade into its throat, and sliced.

Spade took off.

"Spade!" Spencer said.

When Spade didn't stop, when he continued toward Pettenski, Spencer turned to us. "We're moving. Now."

"We have to help them," Dave said.

"They are trained soldiers. They have combat experience. They can take care of themselves. Now move it!" Spencer pointed east. "Now!"

Spade yelled and then jumped into the fight. He kicked over a zombie, dropped a knee onto its back, lifted its head by its hair, and drew his blade across its throat.

My kids saw more than they needed. "Let's go," I said to Dave.

Dave took Sues by the hand.

Allison was crying. I bit my upper lip. There were no words.

Charlene was already following Corporal Spencer.

It didn't feel right leaving two soldiers behind. Did not feel right at all.

# CHAPTER FOUR

On the opposite end of the O'Rourke Bridge were more disabled vehicles. The hood was up revealing the engine compartment of an SUV. One of those small Italian cars was on its side, up on the sidewalk of the bridge. Others were smashed together.

When people inoculated with the vaccination changed into zombies, it happened fast enough. They actually change. How long the incubation period lasted, I had no idea. Like I'd said earlier, seemed like everyone changed on the same day, though, which, when you thought about it, didn't make sense. None at all, but it still felt that way.

"Sergeant, we crossed the bridge. Headed down to the marina now." Spencer waved with his arm. We were taking the Joy Lane footpath. "Yes, sir."

The path led to Marina Drive. The river we'd just crossed, we now headed back toward. Sailboats and yachts filled parking spots in a large lot. The Genesee River emptied into Lake Ontario. It wasn't an oddity, but was one several rivers that ran south to north. There was no mistaking it, as it was muddy brown, and smelly. Some of the larger boats still sat in slips.

"Coast Guard has a boat on the way to get us," Spencer said.

Clouds filled the sky. There might be another storm. At the very least, it was going to rain.

Spencer yelled into his radio, "Spade. Pettenski. Let's go. Let's go!"

I wished I had heard if they answered. The Corporal gave no indication. We didn't stop. "Are they coming?" I said.

"Keep going," Spencer said.

"We can't leave them. They're right there," Dave said, and pointed up at the bridge.

"Spade. Pettenski." Spencer looked intently at Dave, as if he was attempting to say, *I'm trying, I'm trying.*

"We should go back for them," I said.

"The boat's coming."

"It can wait," Dave said. "Sues, you stay here."

I told Allison the same thing. "Watch my kids."

"I cannot let you go," Spencer said. He had no ammo and no grenades, so the only way he could stop us was physically. I had no doubt he could do it, but would he try?

I heard the Coast Guard. The silence around us was shattered by the engine puttering in the river. "We'll be fast," I said.

"Daddy, no," Cash said.

Charlene took his hand. "Hurry back," she said.

Dave and I ran fast. I ignored the stitch in my side and pressed my hand against the pain. It was not going to slow me. The sound of that boat getting closer just screamed salvation.

"We don't have any weapons," Dave said.

I ignored him. We rounded the walk to the bridge and stopped.

Pettenski was down. Zombies were on top of him. They pulled and ripped at his flesh. Spade was about to throw creatures off his comrade. It would be useless at this point.

"Spade," I shouted. "Spade!"

He wasn't going to be able to save Pettenski.

Dave and I ran at them.

Spade looked at us, waved us away.

There were more zombies on the bridge. They took up four lanes, moving like a mob. Slow, sluggish, but deadly.

The milky white skin that glazed their eyes was almost too much to bear. You wanted to look away, close your own eyes and wish them gone, and wish the nightmare over.

"Come with us, Spade," Dave said. "We can't save Pettenski. We can't."

Spade kicked the head of a zombie with combat boots. Must have been steel-toe, because I heard the crunch from where we were.

"Let's go," I shouted. "Now!"

Spade looked torn. "Now, Spade. Now," Dave said.

Perhaps sensing the uselessness, Spade left Pettenski. Pettenski was beyond healing, beyond mending. He was dead.

Spade ran at us with fast zombies chasing after him. Five, no, six of them. The creatures sprinted. Spade didn't have a chance.

I ran toward Spade.

The man had been fighting for over five minutes, puncturing and annihilating a whole host of undead. He was raw, and worn out.

"Knife," I yelled as I got close.

He tossed it; I caught it, and ran past him.

I drove the blade into the closest zombie. It went through the eyeball. The jagged blade sawed into the brain. I shoved my foot into its gut and pulled the knife free. I spun to my right, all the way around, and buried the blade into the throat of another.

Thick black blood oozed from the wound, coating my hand. The zombie pulled back. I lost my grip. The knife was still lodged in place.

The other four zombies were almost on me.

I lunged forward and used both hands to retrieve the weapon just as I was tackled.

It was on me. Up close. Its flesh was purple, and pasty. Those milky white eyeballs. Bits of human flesh wedged between teeth as its mouth opened wide. It looked as if its nose had been chewed off completely. Black gums, rancid breath, and a darting black tongue came at me.

I stabbed it over and over in the back and side, feeling the blade bounce across bone. It had to be doing damage inside, severing things and shredding others.

The zombie seemed unaffected.

It was all about the brain, the central nervous system. It truly was the only way to stop them. Only, I couldn't get at its head.

Its hands wrapped around my throat. I fought with one arm to wriggle free, to no avail. It kept snapping teeth at me, jousting its head forward hard, but my forearm deflected the bites.

It was going to be the end. There were far too many zombies on the bridge. Even if I managed to get away from this one, it would be only a fraction of a second before...

Bullets rang out. A lot of them. A machinegun was being fired.

The zombie on me was pulled off and tossed aside.

Dave huffed and puffed. He was covered in dark blood. He jumped onto the zombie's skull with both feet as I slowly sat up and pushed my way up to stand. That skull shattered. Brain matter squished out from every orifice.

A Humvee was on the bridge, cleaning house.

The gunner on top reminded me of Han Solo in the gun pit of the *Millennium Falcon*. The cavalry arrived.

Dave grabbed my arm, turned me. Spade was down by Joy Lane. We raced toward him. My heart hammered inside my chest. Rolling tears felt cold against my skin. I thought it had been over; my kids would have been orphaned.

Spade waved toward the Humvee, and let out a whoop.

We rounded Joy and cut to Mariana Drive.

I saw the Coast Guard boat docking. My kids ran for it. They didn't yet see me. They didn't look back. Zombies closed in on them.

# CHAPTER FIVE

Spade reached the zombies headed for the Coast Guard first, just as shots sounded. The zombies dropped one by one. None made it to the vessel. None able to harm my kids, Allison, or Sues.

Spencer was on the boat, pulling them in. The river current bounced the vessel up and down. Splashes from the wake crashed over the dock.

We jumped over fallen zombies, ignoring the headshots; the thick black blood oozing from bullet hole sized shattered skulls.

"Second Humvee is up there," Spade said. Spencer nodded. He turned and said something to a crewman.

The revving engine of the Humvee came from behind. As I set a shoe onto the craft, and as Spencer offered down a hand to hoist me up and over, I looked back. Once safely on the ship, I watched.

All the noise. Boats, Humvees, machine guns . . . zombies came from everywhere. Looking up, I saw still more on the bridge. Several climbed over the side and fell lifeless into the river. They wanted us to the point of plunging to a most certain death? They just kept . . . you couldn't say jumped. It was clearly falling. They hated rain, but would water kill them? Could they swim?

I couldn't look away. What started as a few, turned into several, and the further from the bridge we were, the more that went over. It was a wave of infected humans. They plunged into the icy river. It was both a sad and terrifying sight; one that was burned into my mind, a memory I would not be able to lose no matter how hard I tried.

The gunner up top on the Humvee climbed down and opened the back door. A soldier, two guys and a female got out. They looked like we must have just over an hour ago. Terrified. Wide-eyed. Breathless.

The driver and passenger in the military vehicle used their rifles to decimate zombies. None as accurate as Spade, but they killed creatures like there was no tomorrow. In our case, that might not be far from the truth.

There were seven of them, four military and what looked like three civilians, and they all ran for the small Coast Guard vessel. Allison stood next to me, and Cash was holding her hand. The two seemed to have bonded. Charlene stood in front of me, made a twitching motion, like if I didn't have a hand on her shoulder, she might jump off the boat and run to assist in an attempt to help them reach us more quickly.

"Marfione," Spade said. "Where are the others?"

"They didn't make it," Marfione said. "We didn't get a radio transmission, but we found the Humvee. The bodies. Wasn't zombies. Someone opened fire on them. It was a massacre. Must have caught them off guard. I don't know what happened there. No idea."

The civilians climbed onto the vessel first. Allison and I assisted as much as we could. I didn't want to be in the way. Standing around and watching ate at my nerves. All I kept thinking about was Josh, Dave's brother. He'd not been killed by zombies, but by someone with a rifle. Shot and killed for no good reason. It had been senseless. Violent and senseless. I wondered if the same person or group that had killed him was responsible for the attack on the third Humvee? Now was not the time.

When all four military personnel from the second Humvee were on board, Spencer shouted something to the crewman at the helm. The craft bounced and bobbed away from the dock just as a handful of zombies reached the slip.

A crewman with a gun took a few headshots. It didn't deter them. They didn't back away, or run off. At this point, it didn't matter. We were in the water, moving north with the current of the Genesee.

I watched the bridge. All of the zombies pressed against the chest high wall had arms stretched out reaching for us. Fingers wiggled in jerky movements. Then they would be up on the wall and falling over. The splashes were big, but silent. The whine ringing from the Coast Guard's engine drowned out any other sound.

Then I felt it. The sense washed over me. It was the first time in days, weeks, maybe. A total sense of relief. With help from friends, I'd found and rescued my kids and now . . . was it finally safe to feel safe? The military was evacuating us from the area, bound to take us somewhere secure and protected. Life might not ever be the same, but all that kept running through my mind was that we'd made it.

We'd survived.

I knew I was smiling.

Dave looked at me, cocked his head to one side and was smiling, too. We shook hands. A quick hug.

"We're going to be all right," he said. "We're going to be just fine."

The tears shed felt bittersweet. Our journey cost lives. People, friends really, that won't ever be forgotten. Ever. "Thank you, Dave, for everything."

Cash latched onto my leg. I'm sure my flood of emotions confused him. I knelt down.

"Where are they going to take us?" he said.

I shook my head. "I don't know, yet, but somewhere safe, you can be sure of that. We're going to someplace away from all of these monsters."

He bit his lower lip as if he was digesting my words. When he nodded and smiled, I realized it had finally sunk in for him, too.

When I stood up, Charlene took my hand. I loved it. I was surrounded by the people who meant the most to me.

"Come here," I said to Allison. She was not to be left out. She was family.

Sues was silent, though, and looking past me.

I turned to see what held her attention. The three other civilians were huddled close, whispering. Maybe having a similar conversation. The two guys sat on either side of the female. They all sat bent forward with elbows on their knees.

The talking stopped when a female with the Coast Guard knelt between them. She set a medical bag down and opened it up. One of the guys, the white one, rolled up his sleeve. He did it slowly. The black guy in the group watched me.

I saw a bloody forearm and raw meat from a gaping, jagged gash.

The black guy and I locked eyes. He nodded. It was slight. Looked like a way to say, *thank you for your concern, but we're good here. Move along. There's nothing more to see.*

I turned away. Wasn't my business.

Carrying blankets, Marfione walked past us. He handed them out. The black guy wrapped one around the woman's shoulders, the white guy's shoulders, and then did the same with the third for himself.

"You guys want some?" Marfione said. He talked to me. I noticed what was happening. I was addressed, because I was assumed to be *in charge* of my group of people. I hoped I was wrong, because I didn't want it to be that way. Shouldn't be that way. Just like with Dave and Josh--we'd all bond. Eventually.

We all declined. The air was cold. Crisp. It felt invigorating.

I saw the Coast Guard station. It had to be about a mile from the O'Rourke Bridge. We were close. Dare I think it, *sanctuary?*

"What happened to the Border Patrol people, the ones in the helicopter? Are they coming with us?" I said.

Marfione crossed his arms. I expected attitude, the way Spencer first treated us on the Humvee. *Need to know basis* and all of that. "They're not coming with us. They've got a different assignment. More to do. They may meet up later. It's been days. We're still trying to assess everything," he said.

"I can't tell you how good it felt seeing them. When they spotted us," I said.

Marfione just nodded. He understood. "You guys were lucky. We're really not finding many people left. This whole thing, it's kind of out of control. I don't know how we're supposed to fix it."

Fix it. Hadn't given it that much thought. Was there a way to come back from this? As a society?

"So, what's the deal? I mean, where are we headed? We can't be staying at the Coast Guard station. I'm guessing we're going on a trip or something."

"We are. Evacuating the area."

"To somewhere safer?" Allison said. She laced her fingers with mine.

"For the most part. There's an internment camp set up just outside of Fort Drum. State Park. Military occupied it. Secured the area," he said.

"Internment camp?" Allison said.

"Relocation war camps," he said. "Popular in World War II. Mostly along the opposite coast. We took Japanese-Americans, and locked them away," he said. "Pretty much, they were guilty based on heritage. Couldn't be trusted. Some were set up here. In New York and some down south." It was said matter-of-fact. No prejudice in his tone of voice.

"Were they dangerous?"

"Doubt it," he said, smiled. "You know Americans. Knee-jerk reactions become laws."

"We have camps like that here in New York?"

"They've popped up quite-like all over the last few years. Have a lot of nervous politicians in office. Figure they might need a place to lock away hostile people at some point. Not sure if they had *now* in mind. They were thinking the places would be needed eventually, I guess. Amazing insight they have, don't you think?" Marfione removed a pack of cigarettes from his pocket, offered them up.

"I'd love one, if you don't mind," I said.

"I don't. Savor it. Not sure when we'll find a supply to replenish though, you know?"

I thanked him. "I'm Chase McKinney and this is Allison Little. We were--before all of this, well, we were dispatchers at nine-one-one."

"Nice," he said. "Can tell by the uniform shirts."

Always hated the uniform shirts; baby blue itchy material, decorated in para-police collar brass, nameplate and pointless badge. Meant to change out of it at when I was at the apartment Changed the pants, but things had been too hectic. Had a backpack filled with clothing, but left it when we ran from the Humvee. Here I was, Allison, as well, still donned in work shirts, and she in those irritating navy blue pants.

"Lieutenant Marfione. Matthew Marfione. Friends just call me Marf," he said. We shook hands. "Let me go check with Spencer to see what's what. But hey, do me a favor? Guys I just brought in, they're pretty shaken up. If you can welcome them some, might make a world of difference."

"We'll do that, sir," I said.

"Just Marf. And thank you. I mean it. Whatever's going on, this world is a worse place than it once was, if you can believe that. Ranks and shit, it don't mean much anymore. We've got to be more concerned about being humans, helping each other. The times, they demand it." He walked past us.

I stared at my cigarette. I had no way to light it. The lake spray was going to ruin it. If I stuffed it in my pocket, I'd crush it. Regardless, I tucked it behind an ear. It would have to keep. "Want to come with me?" I said.

"You want to go over now?" Allison said.

"He's right," I nodded toward Marf. "Why wait?"

Before we could head over, we started to dock alongside a larger craft. The Coast Guard crew on our vessel yelled to the crewman on the other vessel. Lines were tossed and our ships were drawn together.

"Okay, everyone," Spencer said. "We're going to move from this boat to the other. One at a time. Coast Guard's going to assist. You'll get a life vest once on board. Put it on immediately. Secure it. If you need assistance, Coast Guard will help."

"Guess it will have to wait," I said.

The Coast Guard station was a large, old white house with a red roof. A plaque hung above the front door that read: *Guardians of the Great Lakes.*

"Supplies are loaded," someone shouted. "Let's get everyone onto this ship."

Thunder boomed above us. Through thick grey clouds, I saw a crack of lightning slice the sky.

# CHAPTER SIX

*1432 hours*

The larger Coast Guard vessel was a *47 Motor Life Boat*, which carried thirty-eight people and four crewmen safely. We had nine civilians, seven military, and eight Coast Guard crewmen on board. Twenty-four in all.

Cedar Point State Park was up the St. Lawrence. With the weather getting worse, we were informed we'd be traveling at roughly twenty to twenty-two knots.

The Captain of the Coast Guard station explained all of this. He was still talking. I zoned in and out, trying to mostly pay attention. I just wasn't in much of a mood for a lecture about a boat.

He wore his full get-up. Guess he didn't look at ranks being nonexistent the way Marf did. Different branches. Guess I could expect as much.

"Even if this thing rolls over, it's designed to right itself," Captain Travis Keel said. "And we've done it, during training. Tipped her and rolled her. Not here. Not on this lake. Swells never get that big here. Seven feet was the biggest we've had on Ontario, best I can recall. So you don't have to ask. It works. The life jackets, purely precautionary."

His smile, his laugh--they did little to settle my stomach. The jackets were like ones found on an airplane. Deflated. Pull on the cord, and they inflate. Not sure how big the waves were, but it felt worse below deck.

"We have roughly a five hour voyage ahead. Storm's going to follow us the whole way. We're going to try and stay outside of it, but that will only add time. We're safe. Just isn't going to be the smoothest ride. Regardless, we're safe here. The bunks aren't comfy, but the sheets are clean. I suggest you take advantage of the time and get some rest."

"Thank you, Captain," one of the men from the second Humvee said.

When the Captain went up top, the rest of us stared at the steps as if we expected someone else to come down.

I took a deep breath, remembering what Lt. Marfione had said. "Before we choose bunks," I said, "I want to introduce myself. I'm Chase. My son, Cash, daughter Charlene, and this is my girlfriend. Allison."

"I'm Dave. Dave Rivera, and this is Sues Melia."

The man who'd thanked the Captain stood up. "My name is Tim Chatterton." He had to be about twenty-seven, at least 6'2". He was dark-skinned with a shaved bald head and a thick beard with no mustache.

We all shook hands.

"Were you two cops?" Chatterton said.

"Worked at nine-one-one. Dispatchers," Allison said. *Worked,* she'd said. She understood the gravity of the situation. My shoulders fell. Only had a white t-shirt on underneath or I'd lose the shirt.

The second man waved. "I'm Nicholas Dentino. Nick," he said. Physically fit, also in his early to mid-twenties and resembled a model who posed for clothing ads in magazines. Short dark hair, set jaw and hazel colored eyes.

I waved back. Shouldn't hold it against him, but if he wasn't going to make an effort to shake hands, neither was I. "How's the arm?" I said.

"Healing, hopefully," he said, and snickered. Sounded like he was all right, but to look at him, I'd say he was scared. Guess we all were. No shame in that.

"I'm Crystal Sutton," the woman said. Her shoulder length brown hair was pulled back tight in a ponytail. She had white skin that clearly revealed that she had not spent the summer bathing in sunlight.

With introductions out of the way, an awkward silence ensued. The idea of getting sleep was attractive. Being able to sleep, as the ship tossed back and forth might prove difficult. Part of me wanted to talk and hear their story.

I wasn't as interested in sharing mine, though. Talking was funny that way. Supposed to be give and take. People clam up if it's too lopsided. I call it being cautious.

"You guys know where we're headed?" Chatterton said.

I shook my head. I watched Dentino. He didn't look well. The boat rose and fell on the swells. Might not be as high as seven feet, but they felt huge just the same. "Was told an internment camp. Somewhere in New York."

"By boat? Where could that be?" Crystal said.

"Up the St. Lawrence," I said.

My son yawned.

Hard not to feel like the last nine people who'd been found alive in Rochester? Could we have been it? Was Border Patrol flying around searching for more survivors? Even if they came across some, what then? The Coast Guard station was empty. No crew was left there, and we were cruising on the biggest of their boats.

"I'm going to get some sleep," Chatterton said. He stretched; arms went wide.

"Good call," I said. "Maybe we can talk some more once we get to the camp."

The other three silently nodded, trying to make it look like that would be a great idea. I wasn't buying it though. Not sure why, but they made me uneasy. Might be the way I kept catching Chatterton eyeballing me. Felt like more than a size-up, a once over. The look seemed filled with disdain and I didn't like it.

The bunks were made for one person, if that. Conserving space had been the intent of the thin design. Cash climbed onto one. He patted the mattress. "Sleep here," he said.

I sat beside him. "Want me to lie down with you?"

"Yes," he said.

Charlene gave me a look. "Where am I supposed to sleep?"

"Know what?" I said. "I bet the three of us can fit."

It excluded Allison. Four of us would never fit. No way.

Sues and Dave took one bunk. Spooned. Dave hugged the silent woman tightly. If I needed to find out more about anyone, it was her. She was with our . . . group, if you wanted to think of us in terms of *them and us*. I knew very little about her or her story. There just hadn't been time.

"You guys get in, give me a minute," I said.

"Gonna tuck me in?" Allison said. She smiled.

"You okay?"

"Of course, I am. I'll let it go tonight. You sleep with them. Tomorrow we find a king size bed. You on one side, me on the other, with them sandwiched between us." She mashed her hands together.

Now, I smiled. "Love the idea."

She pulled back the sheets, lay down and pursed her lips.

"What?" I said.

"Can you sneak me a kiss?"

"I can do that," I said, and kissed her.

"Are we going to be okay now? Is the worst over?"

"I want to say, yes," I said.

"But you don't know."

"No. I don't know. We're all together. It's a start, you know. It all seems to be going in a better direction."

She touched my face, forehead, and stared into my eyes. "Go get some sleep. Hug your kids."

"Good night," I said. I knew it was barely 3:00 PM, but I felt exhausted.

I laid down on my back with a kid on either side, their heads and a hand on my chest.

The boat bounced and rocked. Thunder echoed down here like cannons firing. The aluminum must act like an amplifier or something. There was no room on the bunk to move even a fraction of an inch. To make matters worse, I never sleep on my back.

Regardless, I closed my eyes and must have fallen asleep immediately.

# # #

Maybe it was the silence that woke me. My eyes opened. It was dark. Took me a moment to remember where I was. Where *we* were. In the belly of a large ship on Lake Ontario headed for the St. Lawrence. I couldn't have moved if I wanted. Kids were still asleep, using my chest their pillow.

As I was about to close my eyes, trying to grab a bit more sleep, I heard it. A whisper. Someone talking softly, anyway. I recognized the voice, deep, with a little gravel to it. All bass. "It's all I'm saying. Something about all of this, it doesn't add up."

"But what do you mean?" Had to be Nicholas Dentino.

"The flu shots, the ones everyone's been pushing about that swine flu, the H7N9, right? You go into any corner store pharmacy, any doctors' office, they want to give you the shot, right? I was in the military. Joined after high school. We had to get vaccinated for everything. And if we went overseas, there were like three-hundred more shots we needed," Chatterton said.

"Okay, so?" It was the female, Crystal Sutton. I barely heard her.

"So, if the virus that is turning everyone into zombies was in those shots, how come these military and coast guard guys don't have it? How come they're not zombies," he said.

"Because they would have been vaccinated," Dentino said.

"Exactly. No way around it."

I remembered the 9-1-1 call I'd taken. The professor or doctor who claimed responsibility for the mess we were now in. He'd kept rambling on and on about a contamination.

Was the outbreak more limited than first expected?

I'd seen the news. Heard reports. The nation's capital was in shambles.

A contaminated batch would not infect the entire country.

That meant one of two, no, three things. Either more than a single batch had been contaminated--possible and likely, and biting or scratching *did* spread the disease. Or both.

The kid we'd found in the woods by the grocery store, Jay, had been bitten, but he hadn't turned into a zombie. He'd been killed by one. Torn to shreds. Had he been torn to shreds before there had been time for him actually to turn? How long did it take to turn, if in fact people did turn after getting bitten by one of the zombies? With Jay, we didn't really give time for change. We'd buried him.

That changed everything. I'd been taking solace, granted just *some* solace, in the idea that the virus wouldn't spread. That bites were bites. They'd hurt, but heal. Now, I didn't know what to think.

Chatterton was right.

Something did not make sense. Regardless of the spreading, why were these military folks not infected, not walking dead? Could they have been immune to the virus, the vaccination? Or could it be something as simple as they just hadn't been vaccinated against the swine flu yet? Maybe there'd be answers once we reached the internment camp.

"I think, if we get a chance, we should run," Chatterton said.

"And them?" Sutton said.

"Guy's got kids. Nothing against him, but that makes the lot a liability, not an asset. No, we keep this to ourselves. Did you see how those things hate the rain and the way they were falling into the river? I'm going to find me an island. A hideaway. You two think about it. Better the three of us on an island together, than locked away in some *concentration* camp. Don't take too long though. I'm just telling you. Me? I see a chance, I'm out."

There was no falling back to sleep. I felt the heat in my cheeks. If they looked at me, they'd know I was awake, and that I'd heard the entire whispered conversation.

So, my kids and I were a liability, huh? We'd have to see about that, wouldn't we?

Thoughts of sanctuary sank. Nothing was over. If anything, it all just began.

# CHAPTER SEVEN

*2013 hours*

I wanted to talk to Allison. She needed to hear what I'd overheard earlier. Now wasn't the time. Moments ago, the Captain woke us. The nine of us, the civilians, were herded together. The soldiers surrounded us. Might look like they were protecting us, keeping us safe from the sides of the craft, but I wasn't so sure. The storm ended. Not sure how long ago. The waves were constant, but smaller. The thunder quit its ruckus a while back. I hadn't seen a flash of lightning since we'd been on deck.

As I stood there, I thought two things. I really wanted a shower. I had to be raw. The last one was nearly a week ago, and somehow, I'd lost the cigarette Marf had shared with me. That pissed me off.

The rain had stopped. That was upsetting, as well. For obvious reasons, I'd come to love the rain since zombies did not.

I hated feeling suspicious toward everyone around us. Part of me, as much as I hated to admit it, really felt like better days were ahead. Chatterton and his two yanked that strand of hope I'd attempted to hold. I'd keep an eye on them. Although trust had never been established, now respect was sent overboard as well. Fuck him. Fuck them.

Ignorance wasn't my goal, wasn't bliss. Better to know where things stood than relish oblivion. Some people operated fine living lost in the world they've created inside their mind, but not me. The key was being prepared to accept whatever that truth might be. Some looked for answers, but buried their head in the sand because they didn't like what was found. Way I saw it, the truth was essential. Me? I dug and dug until whatever hidden truth was there was unearthed.

"We're on the St. Lawrence now," Captain Keel said. "Made pretty good time, actually."

Something had to be wrong with the Captain. Guy was always smiling. He didn't look at one person too long. His eyes roamed back and forth over each of us. When they were on me, I didn't like it, even before I'd listened in on Chatterton's conspiracy theory.

"Be roughly forty minutes or so and we'll be at Cedar Point Park. Don't know about you all, but I'm hungry and looking forward to a nice meal. We're getting in late. I radioed ahead this morning, and told them to expect us late tonight. Keep the kitchen open, and such. I was assured dinner would still be hot once we docked." Captain Keel stood with his hands clasped behind his back. The waves were big enough that I'd lose my balance if I mimicked his stance.

I wasn't sure what was expected of us. We stood there for what seemed to go on for a while. Soldiers held their rifles. I noticed full magazine clips on their belts. I don't remember giving back the sidearm. All I knew was I no longer had it.

The tension must have been thick, because no one talked. We all seemed to sense . . . *it*. No idea what 'it' was. Don't know how I felt about docking. We were clearly safer on water. There was that movie. Costner was in it. A world with no land. Floating cities built on boats. Might be a viable alternative, once I figured out if zombies could swim or not. If they just didn't like water, or water harmed them. Throw buckets of water on them, listen to them screech and watch them melt. That would make everything simple. So simple.

Cash squeezed my hand. I looked down. He looked to his right, pointed. I followed with my eyes. Land.

Felt like we'd completed a journey across an ocean. Left America for some unknown, uncharted location. We'd spent over four hours on a lake I'd swum in since I was kid. We'd met the St. Lawrence River, and although Canada was a hell of a lot closer, we were still in New York. Go figure. Makes you feel kind of small and unimportant. And it was just a lake. A big one, but still just a lake.

"When can we take these off?" Charlene tugged at her life vest.

"Careful of that pull-string. Those things swell up fast. Feel like it's choking you," I said.

"Can we take them off?"

The boat still swayed. While the idea of a meal sounded amazing, my stomach might not agree. Nauseated and rumbling, I felt pretty sure I'd puke up whatever I sent down. "Not just yet," I said.

"Dad," she said. "What do you think they'll do with us once we get there?"

"It'll be fine," I said. The question filled my mind. I'd worried about what might be waiting for us, too. Might just be the thought of a camp designed to detain people that got to me most. We'd done nothing wrong, except survive. We weren't prisoners, or detainees. It still felt that way.

Crystal Sutton looked down at my daughter, then up at me. Smiled. I looked away. Wasn't in the mood for games. The smile meant shit. I was a liability to them.

I found Chatterton, locked my stare on his. Our eyes narrowed. Don't think it was me being all paranoid. There was a question to his expression. Saw it clearly. Did he suspect I'd been awake and whether I'd heard everything said?

It was something. Might as well be that.

Let him wonder.

"Let's go over here," I said, and never looked away from Chatterton. Using my hands and arms to guide my people, yes, I thought it . . . my people . . . to one side of the vessel where there were places for us to sit.

"Are you going to tell me what's going on?" Allison said.

"Ah, yeah. What was that? What was that all about?" Dave held onto Sues' hand. I don't think I've seen him *not* touching her since the Humvee rescued us. Never heard them talk, but they were always touching.

Chatterton, Sutton and Dentino were close. The boat was big, but not so big we could be alone. Nevertheless, with the waves, and the crewmen working, I didn't think they could overhear us if I decided to retell what I'd heard. Question was, did I talk in front of the kids, or wait?

Waiting might not be an option, though. Opportunities alone might become less and less frequent. Having them five or six feet away might be the most privacy we'd get to experience for *who knows how long*.

I also had to think about Chatterton and about what he'd said.

My kids. They made me, us, a liability.

"*We're* family now," I said. They leaned closer. Maybe it was the tone of my voice, or a look on my face. I felt it the moment I spoke. It was a *This Is The Shit* talk. We all knew it. "*Us*. The six of us are family now and we need to watch each other's backs. Okay?"

"Are you going to tell us what happened? What do you know that we don't?" Dave grit his teeth. I liked it. Guy was more like me than I'd thought when we first met. Answers. Truth. It's what he sought, too. No one had time for bullshit. Not anymore.

"When we were below deck, I woke up. I heard the other three talking."

"What did they say?" Allison said.

I told them everything.

# CHAPTER EIGHT

Dentino collapsed. He just, *plop*, went down.

"Sergeant, Sergeant!" Marfione said, and then ran toward Dentino.

The woman who had bandaged his arm yelled, "Don't touch him!"

"But Erway…"

"Stand back," she said. She put a hand on Marf's chest and pushed. "Back."

Erway didn't have a medical bag this time, but wore a patch on her uniform. It identified her as a Coast Guard paramedic. "Captain? Captain Keel, have the civilians go back below."

I didn't like being ushered away. We were not cattle, so no one was herding us. "What's wrong with him?"

"Take your kids and go below," she said, and stood toe to toe with me, her nose an inch from mine. The authority was there. The threat obvious. I wouldn't have cared if she'd held a gun to my head. I would take my kids below deck, because I wasn't sure what might happen next.

Not because I was being ordered.

"Sir," a crewman said.

"Yeah," Captain Keel said. He didn't look to see who called out to him. His eyes were locked on Dentino. His tongue kept licking his lips. *Where's your stupid smile now, eh, Captain?*

"Still can't reach anyone at the camp. No one."

45

Keel turned. I saw it in his eyes. If he could have shot the crewman, he would have. Guessing the fact that they couldn't reach anyone at the camp was meant to be a secret.

"Try again," Keel said.

"Have been. Nothing. I mean nothing. Static."

"Storm might have knocked out the repeaters." Captain Keel said, the smile back. Our, ever-smiling and optimistic leader, attempted reassuring everyone with a look. Don't think it fooled a single one of us. Didn't fool me. I'd caught a glimpse of Keel. An uncensored glance into who this man was.

"Excuse me, what?" It was Sergeant Landon Vitale. "You can't reach anyone at the camp?"

The crewman looked at Keel, as if for permission to answer. "That's right, sir."

"But you said 'still.' Makes me think this isn't something you're just learning," Vitale said. "What happened to the nice hot meal, and them keeping the kitchen open? That they were expecting us?"

"Please, downstairs everyone, so Lieutenant Erway can help her patient." Keel waved hands back and forth. It looked like he thought he could dismiss us, make us vanish with a wave of those liver-spotted hands. "This patient is sick."

"When was he bitten?" Erway said.

I thought she'd been talking to me. I opened my mouth, but then closed it.

Chatterton was kneeling beside Dentino. "I don't know. A day ago. Two. Wasn't much of a bite. Teeth barely broke the skin."

"But the skin had been broken," Erway said. Didn't sound like a question.

Chatterton looked up at me. I had my kids behind me. Dave by my side. Was he somehow blaming me for this? It's what his eyes said. That would be ludicrous. Might just be pure resentment in his stare. Again, ludicrous, but it was there. I wasn't imagining it. Unless…unless it was shame. Anger and shame.

"Yes," he said. "The skin was broken. We cleaned it real good. Poured stuff on it to kill germs. That clear stuff? I forget what it is called."

"Hydrogen Peroxide?" Erway used a pen light and flashed it into Dentino's eyes.

"That's right. It bubbled, turned white, so we figured we'd cleaned it good. Then we bandaged it. Didn't take more than a couple of Band-Aids, and we wrapped it in gauze, too."

Dentino foamed at the mouth and his back bucked. His arms went out wide, palms against the deck, fingers spiked like spider legs. He shook, as if having a seizure.

It was in a million horror movies. The change.

"Sergeant," Erway said.

There was a lot of confusion. Soldiers moving about. Some yelling. I couldn't follow everything happening.

"Captain, how long have you been out of radio contact with the camp?" Sergeant Vitale said.

"Not now, Sergeant," Keel said.

Erway looked up from her patient. "Sergeant, I need your soldiers. Now."

Vitale stared at the Captain, but motioned at his men. They trained weapons on Dentino. The guy wasn't going anywhere. That's clearly what Erway wanted. She must not trust Dentino's condition. Must feel threatened by him.

If he changed into a zombie, he was as good as dead, again, anyway. Spade leveled his sidearm, finger on the trigger, one eye closed, arms extended. Yes, Dentino was as good as dead.

I kept going back to Jay. Would he have turned if we hadn't of buried him? Had he turned and come back as a zombie, but was now buried in a shallow grave with no way out? Looking at Dentino, foaming, seizing, I think Jay's death played out better. I don't know what I would have done had he changed.

"I want the civilians down below," Captain Keel said. "The military has this. They are going to handle it. They don't need an audience."

Handle this? An audience for what?

"You're not killing him," Chatterton said. "He's sick. You can see it. He's just sick. He's not; he isn't one of those things. He didn't die. He's not dead. Zombies…they were once human, died and then return from the dead. That hasn't happened here."

"This isn't a movie," Erway said. "Those are rules created by Hollywood."

"He just needs help. Doctor, you have to help him," Chatterton said. He held his hands clasped together in front of him.

Erway shook her head. "I'm not a doctor. You dressed the wound, but it still got infected. I don't know what more we can do for him."

Dentino groaned, sounding like he was in pain. Figured his body was in the midst of a transformation. His blood, organs, muscles, and tissue attempted to fight off whatever disease had been transmitted.

"Captain," a crewman said. "We're about to dock. I don't see anyone. No one."

I looked to the side of the ship. The coast we'd been following widened. There were at least twenty boating slips. This vessel was too big to fit into any of them except the one on the end.

The land itself was covered in fog. The cold and warm air, the storm, all perfect make-up for fog. Thick, it didn't move. It just sat there, like a natural layer on green grass, and formed leafless trees. The light poles along the shore by the docks cast an iridescent glow over everything.

Everything happening screamed B-Horror film. Zombies and fog, and Dentino about to go from the living to the undead. I mean, what the fuck? Erway might have tried to distance this reality from Hollywood, but I wasn't buying it.

"I need you to move away from him," Erway said.

Chatterton's hand shot out. He took a fistful of Erway's uniform at the shoulder.

Weapons cocked and the uniform clicking of them made me stare around at the military. I didn't know if they were marines, army, or what. They wore nothing that gave that away. I never thought to ask. Didn't matter then; still didn't now.

"Release her," Vitale said. "Now. Then, do as she said. Back away from the man."

It didn't look like Chatterton meant his reaction to be threatening, but was clearly taken that way. I didn't see it as such, though. The guy would never do well playing poker. His every emotion was visible in his eyes. His feelings were displayed through them as if a neon sign.

"I just want you to try to help him," he said.

"Release the Lieutenant. Do you hear me? I will not ask again." Vitale did not take any steps closer. Wouldn't need to. Six armed soldiers punctuated his threat.

Chatterton let go of Erway. His fingers rolled into a loose fist. Nothing angry about it. "Please, just see what you can do."

I hadn't realized it, but Dentino's body relaxed at some point. He was flat on his back. His hands still gripped at nothing. His eyes were open. Not blinking.

It might be too late, I thought, too late to do anything more.

"Back away," Erway said. She sounded heartless and cold. Agitated.

Chatterton went from kneeling to standing in one smooth motion and took two steps back. Spade holstered his gun, grabbed the black man by the arm, spun him around and walked him to the back of the vessel.

"Docking sir," the crewman said.

The drama unfolding held everyone's attention. I don't think I'd noticed Cash's hands gripping my leg, his fingers squeezing my skin beneath the material.

I didn't know what to do. Sheltering him made the most sense. He was nine. Just nine. But I didn't want to go below. I needed to see what happened. I needed, not to witness, but understand. What were we up against?

What were the rules?

But he was nine.

Once Chatterton was away, soldiers now in front of him, Erway lowered her head. She listened for breathing. Her ear was an inch or so from Dentino's mouth.

I turned around. "You stay up here," I said to Dave.

"I'm staying," Charlene said.

I let her.

Allison and I took Cash down the stairs, back to the bunks.

"Is that man going to die? Is he going to become a zombie?" Cash said. "Are the soldiers good people, or bad?"

I had the same questions, and answers to none of them.

I lifted my son into my arms and sat on the bunk, Allison beside me.

"What do we do?" she said.

We all had questions, and the fear was evident in each one.

*What do we do?*

A gun fired. Cash wrapped his arms tighter around my neck. I wasn't sure I'd be able to breathe.

The gunshot wasn't loud down here, but we heard it. No mistaking what it had been. I waited for more. I counted to ten, but nothing else.

Allison had her hand on my knee. A tight, tight grip.

Dave came down the stairs. His skin was pale.

Sues walked down behind him. Once below, they held hands again. I gave them a look. I was about to ask where Charlene was, when she came down last.

"Dentino was sick," Dave said. "We thought he died. Erway checked for a pulse. He didn't have one. No sooner had she stood up, he sat upright. Bolted upright. His eyes were...they were like *their* eyes, you know. And that one guy, the one who'd walked Chatterton away, he did it."

*What do we do?*

A valid question. I'd made assumptions. All along, I'd been making them. Guesses that I believed. I made them seem plausible, possible, and probable. I'd fooled myself. I figured the zombies here was all there would be. Eventually, humanity could step up and wipe them out, once we got a handle on the situation. Once the initial shock ended. Once the survivors gathered and unified.

"Here's the thing, Chase. I think we were the only ones who were surprised that he changed into one of those things. I couldn't tell, but it was almost like the others. They seemed to expect it."

"Can't be. If Erway thought he was going to turn, they would have isolated him. They wouldn't have let him down here with us," I said.

"They wouldn't have?"

I shook my head, but didn't say a thing. Couldn't, because I wasn't positive. Thought about what Chatterton and his group talked about before everyone went to sleep. Why weren't these particular military people zombies? The military is huge on vaccinating the shit out of its boys. Sounded so sarcastic, but in a time of crisis, who can you count on if not the military?

*What do we do?*

They'd get hungry and die off. The vaccination itself would gradually kill them. Undead would have to go back to being dead at some point. The virus already infected all those that could ever be infected through the vaccinations. It wouldn't spread. It couldn't spread. It couldn't get worse.

*What do we do?*

I had the answer.

We don't get bitten, that's what. We don't get scratched and we don't get bitten.

# CHAPTER NINE

*Cedar Point State Park--NY Interment Camp, 2120 hours*

Captain Keel ordered everyone back up on deck. Lieutenant Marfione gathered us, ushered us to the stairs.

"What's going on?" I said. We needed answers and it was about time we got them. At this point, we deserved them. Being kept in the dark wasn't going to cut it.

"I'm not sure, but I don't like it," Marf whispered. It was honest. I respected that. "Just stick together. We're all in this, you know what I mean?"

"I do," I said. "Thank you."

We climbed the stairs. Couldn't get closer if we'd been medically joined. Lights on the vessel helped. The boat seemed to be hovering in mist. Not floating on the river. The mist moved like water, rolling all around.

Sergeant Vitale stood among the six Coast Guard crew, along with Lieutenant Erway, and their captain. They were up by the helm. We filed in and faced them. They'd have to talk down to us. Had to be on purpose. A power play.

Cash and Charlene were in front of me. Allison, Dave and Sues stood beside me. Chatterton and Crystal were side-by-side. Spade, Spencer and Marfione huddled together, with hands on their rifles. Three other military people we hadn't yet met were shoulder to shoulder by the edge of the boat.

I needed to know where everyone was, help keep track of things. Might be OCD. Could be, I just didn't like surprises.

Keel cleared his throat. "Military is going to explore the compound. We've lost all radio contact. We've not seen any signs of people, or zombies for that matter. We need to know what's happening out there before we all get off the boat."

"What do you think is going on?" It was Dave. He'd raised his hand, but didn't wait to be called on. I wanted to tell him this wasn't school. We weren't a part of any military branch, and the time for raising our hands before speaking had passed days ago, but I didn't. Raising a hand seemed like the kind of thing that made Dave more comfortable, so let him.

"As soon as we know more, we'll share that information," Keel said. It was a snap-answer. Curt. Perhaps meant to dissuade questions.

"That wasn't what he asked. He wanted to know, we all want to know, what *you* think is going on," I said.

"Sir," Keel said.

"Chase," I said. "Chase McKinney."

"Mr. McKinney, I wasn't avoiding the question. Truth is that I don't have an answer. I have no clue what's going on. I'm not going to guess. Guessing doesn't get us anywhere. It doesn't help the situation one bit. What will help is actual intel. The longer we stand here talking about it, the longer it takes the soldiers to go and bring back actual, helpful and factual information."

"Captain," I said. "If the internment camp has been breached, the soldiers could be walking into a mess."

"It's what they're trained for, Mr. McKinney. Now, please, can we let them do their jobs?"

"Sir," Spencer said. "Do you know anything about the layout? That would help. I mean, anything you do have, we'd appreciate it."

Keel removed his captain's hat. Using both hands, he held it in front of his chest. "What I know is that the compound is surrounded by chain-link fence. Coiled barbed wire ran along the top. There is supposed to be watchtowers in each corner."

A prison. It's what it sounded like. Once inside, there was no getting out, unless allowed out. How long ago was it that this particular facility had been constructed? Why keep it all this time? Who was it the government worried they might have to incarcerate?

"Inside the fence?" Spencer said.

"Inside, what I've been told, there are roughly thirty houses. Each about twenty-by-one-hundred. Four —what they called them— apartments in each."

"That's a hundred and twenty homes we have to clear?" Spade said.

"Way I understand it, there are no walls between apartments. Imaginary lines are what have been explained. Each apartment is twenty-by-twenty-five feet. Tight living quarters, but it's a camp, not meant to be luxurious, not by any means. There are also three separate mess halls. Buildings where people could congregate to eat, or hold meetings. There are also four military barracks, and a central stage area. The military barracks are at the four corners of the compound. The stage and mess halls are in the center. There is a mobile army surgical hospital. I believe it is also centrally located."

"How many people are supposed to be here already?" Spade said.

"Roughly seventy. Between military, medical and civilian personnel."

Vitale stepped forward. "I want three volunteers to explore the compound."

Dave, along with six soldiers, raised their hand.

"Palmeri, Barron, Saylor, you three will maintain radio contact the entire time. Do not engage any hostiles if it can be avoided. Scope out the perimeter first. If you need to enter, enter. Gather as much information as you can, and then get back here. Is that understood?"

In unison, "Sir, yes, sir."

"I'd like to go as well, sir," Dave said. He sounded all military. Deep voice. Showed courage.

Chatterton stared at me. First time I couldn't figure out what thoughts spun around inside his skull. Either he wanted me to rein in my guy, or he thought Dave's volunteering was commendable. Couldn't tell. Not for sure. It was one or the other, that much I was certain.

"That won't be necessary," Vitale said.

"I don't want you to go." Sues might have thought she whispered, but she hadn't. The one arm at his side had both her hands wrapped around the wrist.

"I think I should," Dave said.

"And I appreciate your bravery, but our soldiers are going to handle this."

"We want our guns back," Dave said.

"They were never your guns," Vitale said.

Dave opened his mouth, but this time, I grabbed his arm. "Not now," I said. No sense getting in a pissing match. Military wasn't just going to hand over weapons. There had to be more on the vessel. More than just what we'd seen, with the soldiers and Coast Guard crew carried. Had to be, because if there wasn't, we might be in some serious, serious trouble.

The three soldiers got off the boat, disappearing into the foggy mist. We gathered around Vitale's radio. The remaining three soldiers seemed ready to spring into action. Any kind of action. They seemed upset that they hadn't been picked to explore.

*That* was a soldier.

Even before the first transmission, we heard it. Not from the radio, but an echo in the distance. The gunfire was one thing. I had no problem with that. None. Unrealistic at this point in time not to expect it. Didn't need to send out a recon team to realize the camp was fucked up.

It was an agonizing shrill. Someone screamed. And screamed. And screamed.

# CHAPTER TEN

The radio crackled.

"Sergeant, Barron's down. He's down!"

"Where are you, Palmeri?" Vitale held the radio in a fist. He backed away from us. No way was he taking this call in private. Safe to say we shared a vested interest.

Spade, Marf and Spencer checked the weapons. They mumbled, so I couldn't make out what each said to the other. It was like a different language.

I smelled smoke, even though I didn't see any. Tough to differentiate anything from the thick fog and the darkness. I kept a hand on each child. Allison was close to my back, her hand on my shoulder. "We need weapons, Sergeant."

"No one else is leaving the boat," Captain Keel said. "We're going to shove off. Get away from the dock."

"You're not going anywhere," Vitale said.

"Didn't say we were, just not staying in this slip. We're going to float out some. Safe distance. Drop anchor. We're safe on the boat," the captain said.

"You're staying," Vitale said. "You're staying right here. My soldiers are out there. We're not leaving them."

"This is my ship. I'm captain. *Me*. I have my crew to th—"

"Don't even say it." Vitale invaded personal space. Keel didn't back down, didn't step away. "My soldiers are out there and we're going after them. When we return, this ship is right here. Where it was when we left it. Do you understand? Am I clear?"

"Sergeant, if you get off my ship, then that is your prerogative. I can assure you we will not still be tied up. We will not abandon you. It is not safe staying right here. There are more lives at stake than the three soldiers. We have eight civilians to think of. We cannot forget about them," he said.

The way he said it. *We cannot forget about them.* I didn't like it. They were privy to something. Not sure what, but it was there in the way he said it.

The breakdown consisted of a struggle. It was over power and fear. Loyalty and commitment. And possibly mission. Keel sounded like a chickenshit to me. Initially.

I couldn't argue with the logic, though. I wanted my kids safe. I wasn't worried about me. I wanted my *family* safe.

"I'm going with you," I said. Sergeant Vitale stared at me.

"Daddy, no!" Cash kept arms wrapped around my leg.

"I have to," I said. "Your sister is going to protect you. She can do that. I know she can."

She didn't smile at me. I knew she appreciated the words, the trust. The boat was going to leave the dock. It would be out on the water. Away from any possible zombie attack. They'd be safe. Charlene wouldn't have to do much more than hold her brother's hand. She could do that. No doubt.

"You're not going," Allison said.

"I'm going with you," Dave said.

"He's not going, Dave," she said. "So you're not going with him. Neither of you is going anywhere."

"We have more weapons," Vitale said. "Spade, arm the men. Leave some rifles and handguns for the Coast Guard."

"We have our own," Keel said. "And we are not going to arm the civilians, Sergeant. They've not been trained. Could be more dangerous giving these women guns…"

"Excuse me?" Sues had fists planted on hips. "That was uncalled for. Out of line. You might be the captain of this ship, but you just made it known that you are a sexist pig. A pig!"

Dave wrapped an arm around her and whispered into her ear.

"Did you hear what he said," she said. She shook a fist at Keel.

Yeah. I *liked* this woman. She clearly was family. Dave had himself a keeper in my eyes.

Spade returned. He dragged a chest, popped the lock and lifted the lid.

"I'll need one," Charlene said.

Spade looked at me and I nodded. "She's tough."

"You know how to use this?" He held out a handgun. Without waiting for an answer, he explained in four steps how to use it. "You turn the safety off like this. Hold the gun out like so. Close one eye and aim. You line this little tab up with what you want to hit. You pull the trigger here. It's that easy."

Cash looked up at me. "Do I get one?"

"Your sister will protect you," I said, again.

Allison, Sues and Crystal took rifles.

"Here's how you load them," he said. First, he showed the ladies, giving them extra ammunition and then he showed Charlene. He gave her a handful of clips.

Chatterton stood quiet. He hadn't volunteered. He hadn't opted out.

"I do not want these people going with you," Keel said to Vitale. "Do you hear me, Sergeant? I will file a formal complaint…"

"With whom, Travis? Huh? Who the fuck you going to file a complaint with? Other than you, the people on this boat, and me, who the fuck you been in contact with? I'd like to know. I really would. Because, my satellite phone hasn't heard shit from anyone. No one. You going to tell my Commander in Chief? Because even if that little fuck is holed up in some fallout bunker, I don't think he's going to give two shits if I handed out some fucking handguns. Is he? You think he's going to care? Answer me! I'm not talking just to fucking talk. Fucking answer me!"

Spade, who had been kneeling by the chest, rose to his feet and in one fluid motion was in front of and moving his sergeant away from conflict. "Sarge," he said.

Vitale shrugged off the soldier's hands. He spun. We locked eyes. "You shoot before?"

"Yes," I said. This was not about being a hero. It's what was right. The right thing to do. I didn't want to go. I needed to. Had to.

"And you?" he said.

Dave nodded.

"What about you?" Vitale stared at Chatterton. "I haven't heard you fucking go peep."

"I'm going with you, sir."

"That's what I wanted to hear. You shoot?"

"Yes, sir."

"They all set, Spade?" Vitale said.

Spade handed the three of us more weapons. Rifles, side arms, extra clips and a big knife, which I clipped the sheath of to my belt.

"You be safe," Charlene said, hugging me.

"I will. You take care of them. Allison, too. But you listen to her. You got me? You're not a kid anymore."

"I know that. We'll be okay."

"I know *that*," I said. I kissed her. Been a long time since she'd let me. Always gave me the top of her head or a cheek. I'll not forget when she was younger. Used to carry her everywhere. People thought something must be wrong with her legs. We were inseparable. At a Fourth of July picnic one year, my uncle took photographs. Told us to smile. Said he didn't have any of us together. Sarcasm dripped from his words. Times changed. As she got older, we remained close, but not as close.

It was bound to happen. Might have been gradual, but noticeable. I felt it. Didn't mean she loved me less. Meant she needed me less. That's what hurt.

"Daddy," Cash said, reaching for me.

Allison took his hand. She knew if Cash got his hands on me, the good-bye would last too long. "We'll be fine. Just remember, no heroics. I mean it," she said.

"I'll be back," I said to both of them. To all three of them.

Sues wasted no time; she stood on tiptoes and kissed Dave on the lips. Most I'd heard her say had been her yelling at our *fearless* captain. She and Dave, they hit it off though. Think desperate situations formed fast bonds. There was a textbook name for it. Two people in a crisis oftentimes fall in love. Crisis ends, isn't long before whatever relationship was started is also over. Different circumstances, I would have busted his chops and given him a hard time. Instead, when he looked at me, I nodded.

We got off the boat. Vitale looked back. Keel stared at us, at him. Neither looked away.

# CHAPTER ELEVEN

*2248 hours*

"You said your satellite phone isn't reaching anyone," I said.

Vitale looked at me. "It's pockets of people. Just pockets. And no one in New York, best we can tell."

"We saw D.C. on the news a few days ago."

"Gone. Virus hit them hard. Everyone and their mother were vaccinated," he said.

"The president?"

"To be honest, I haven't heard a word, but I'm a sergeant, so not very high on the totem pole," he said. "He wasn't vaccinated. Vice president either. I'm sure they're in hiding somewhere secret and separated. To be honest, he's no one now, just a survivor like you or me, but he has a fancy as shit bunker to wait it all out in. That's the difference."

"So what was this? This facility? I mean, if there's no government..."

"Never said there was no government. Just a lot fewer of them, is all. Hell, they needed some serious down-sizing anyway." He laughed in a short, guttural burst. "This camp is military. Medical. What we were told almost a week ago is that they're set up around the country. Going to be used for research. A way to find a cure to un-infect the diseased."

"We were going to be guinea pigs?"

"Blood samples only. It isn't asking much. Doctors need clean blood to work on ways to fight the virus, which is an oxymoron, since a vaccination against a virus was what caused it all in the first place. Point is, if you didn't get inoculated, your blood is prime real estate."

"But, I mean, I thought I heard it was a contaminated vial that impacted a shipment of vaccinations that got sent out, so a case full of people were given the medicine. However many vials are in a shipment, or a case. I don't get why this is so widespread," I said, knowing my desperation for answers was transparent as shit.

"You heard wrong. The vaccinations against the H7N9 were contaminated. Not every shipment, but most. Apparently, the vial that broke wasn't immediately discovered. The contaminant was in the air, fouling up shit for nearly twenty-four hours before someone spotted broken glass under one of the workstations. That stuff…that contaminant…managed to find its way into everything. Went out in shipments across the country. The entire country and this is where it gets worse -- overseas. I have no idea what kind of fucked-up shit's going on in Europe, but I can bet it ain't any prettier over there than it is over here," Vitale said.

I stared at him.

He stared back.

"You knew. The military knew."

"We got word about the vaccination issues, but as they say, far too late. The elderly, the young, they were first in line. Most first responders, your firemen, police officers, paramedics and a good portion of the military, too were in trouble and we knew it. What we *didn't* know, couldn't know, was the side effects. That. This. These zombies. No one knew."

"Holy fucking shit. You knew. Most of the military spared?" Dave said.

"Most? No, they were not, son."

"And what happened to them." I pointed toward the camp. "To everyone here?"

"We're about to find out."

I had numerous questions that I wanted answered, but now wasn't the time. I only prayed there would be time later. It felt like there might not be and that worried me.

"Look, I'm leaving one of you here. Right fucking here," Vitale said. He pointed a finger and jabbed it toward the captain, "That fucker tries to move the boat, you shoot him. Fucking headshot."

"Sir?" Marf let his eyes move from the captain to his sergeant. "You're not serious, sir?"

"The fuck I'm not. When we left the port, when we all climbed onto the vessel there, Captain Travis up there, he hadn't heard shit from the camp. In hours. How long it take us to get here? Like four five hours. And nothing from the camp. The whole time. Nothing. Got the crewman up there trying to reach someone. Anyone. Think that fucking captain shared any of that information with *us*? He didn't. Not with you and not with me. So we boated all the way the fuck out here, and we now I've got three soldiers out there. And fuck if I have heard from them in, how long, Spade?"

"About six minutes," he said.

"Six fucking minutes of radio silence since we heard about Barron. Six fucking minutes. So yeah, I'm serious as shit. Keel tries to pull away from the dock, blow the fuckers brains all over his own damned deck." Sergeant Vitale grit his teeth. He knew Keel heard every word. Wanted it known not as a threat, but a promise.

"I'll stay," Spencer said.

"You can do it, soldier?"

"Kill that captain? Yes, sir." Spencer stood at attention.

Vitale nodded. "This is your command. You protect those people on board. We'll keep in touch as best we can. We're going to operate under radio silence as best we can. Everyone understand?"

"Yes, sir," we said.

"Fine, you can at-ease. Just keep your eyes open, got me? Watch the boat, the water and the land. This fog is going to be tough as shit seeing much of anything," Vitale said.

"I understand, sir."

I felt all Secret Service-*like*; radio buds in my ears, a button to depress for speaking into the cuff. Kinda cool.

"Emergency transmissions only," the sergeant reiterated. "And you, Corporal, you understand everything I've said?"

"Clearly, sir."

"Okay. We're going to split up into two search parties. Lieutenant Marfione, you're going to take McKinney and Rivera. Chatterton, you're going to come with Private First Class Spade and me."

Vitale used our last names, symbolized to me that we're together, a team.

"Headshots people," Vitale said. "Be smart about your resources. If you can stab 'em without getting bitten, do it. Saves ammo and is quieter. These bastards are drawn to noise. And McKinney, Rivera, you do whatever Marf tells you to do without question. Do you understand?"

"Yes, sir," we said.

"We don't have much to go on. We're assuming Barron is injured at best. The three of them might be hobbling around inside the compound. Look at who you are shooting before you shoot them. Not gonna have minutes, or even seconds to contemplate what to do. Split decisions, okay? Might be Palmeri, but now she's got lifeless fucking eyes, and she is drooling black blood all over her uniform. Might think she was a cool soldier, but now she's a zombie. What do we do then, Spade?" Vitale said.

"Headshot."

Vitale clapped his hands together. "Bingo. Headshot. However, if she is just covered in blood and guts from fighting zombies, then we want to try our best not to blow her fucking brains out. Clear?"

"Yes, sir," I said. It sounded comical, like a joke. This was Robin Williams improving a speech to troops. Might have come across better had he started with a big, *Gooooood morning, Apocalypse!* At the very least, a *Na-nu na-nu.*

Sorry. Wasn't liking it. Vitale and Keel, our leaders, were losing it. Out of control. I didn't know if it was nervous breakdowns, if they'd been exposed to other chemical agents, or what. Their...behavior was obscure and uncomforting.

Dave stared at me. He agreed. Was in his eyes. We'd have to have each other's backs. Chatterton looked our way. No doubt. The three of us saw a problem. If I wasn't reading the signs wrong, Marf also felt the same. Trust was thin in these . . . platoons. Getting thinner by the second.

Spade? Spencer? They acted gung-ho for Vitale. Didn't mean they agreed with or were against anything unfolding, just I hadn't seen anything to indicate one side was preferred over the other. Except Spencer was ready to shoot a Coast Guard Captain, and Spade was ready to explode the brains of a fellow soldier on a split-second guess.

Other than that...

# # #

I did not like leaving my kids on the boat. It was the very last thing I wanted to do, but there didn't seem to be much choice. People were in trouble. They'd saved us. My kids were safer with the vessel. I had every intention of returning.

Clouds back lit by moonlight looked iridescent in the sky. When they passed over the moon, we were plunged into darkness, but they passed quickly. The fog seemed to be settling some, too. It stayed low around our calves and as we walked, it swirled away and returned.

Staying low, we walked several hundred yards away from the ship. I saw chain link fence and a tall wooden structure at the corner.

"Watch tower," Marf said. "The entrance to the camp should be on the north side."

Our breath plumed from our mouths with each quick and shallow breath then fell behind us. It reminded me of puffs emitted from old train engines. Felt more like a wolf out on a winter night. We resembled a pack; crouched and hunting.

"Once we get in, Marf, you three go right. West. We'll go east. Do a perimeter check. Listen for anything. Then we'll start clearing the apartments, working our way to the center. Easiest thing is going to be following Palmeri, Pettenski and Saylor's footprints. Mud's good for something," Vitale said.

We followed in a row. All the rain softened the earth; wet the dirt. My dress shoes were shit in this mud. The goo gathered on the soles. I walked carefully, afraid I might lose one or worse, both. Cash was more of a gamer than I was. He liked his war games best. I'd played with him more than once. Once would have been enough. While he controlled his soldier with ease, mine always seemed stuck in one place, spinning in circles with the weapon aimed at either the sky or the ground. Can't imagine playing a game would help now, but it did feel eerily similar. I was out of my element.

Through the fence, I could see the apartments. They were not big, but long. I saw no signs of life. I wondered how many people were supposed to be here, uninfected, military and medical.

Vitale's words spun around in my head while we walked. I understood the basics. Testing the uninfected for cures. Can't imagine the entire population gone, walking dead. The idea was surreal. Pockets of uninfected left? Pockets. The idea overwhelmed, depressed and I needed to block it off, file it away, and worry about it later.

We rounded a corner by the second watchtower. The fence seemed to go on forever, disappearing into darkness. We had come upon the entrance to the camp soon, had to. I looked up; saw the bottom barrel rolls of barbed wire. I'd thought it early, that the place felt like a prison. Now it seemed like we were about to break into one.

Best guess, something got in or was already infected on the inside. Hated guessing, but was all that made sense. Still -- where was everyone?

This brought me back to my first question. How many people had been here to begin with, before we arrived?

# CHAPTER TWELVE

*0108 hours*

The front gate was wide open. I don't know what I expected. I thought it might be off hinges, or a cut chain with a smashed padlock disassembled on the ground. No, there was none of that. The gate was just open.

"Okay," Vitale said. "Footprints look fresh. Split in three different directions. Looks like they separated. First mistake. I find them; I've got some ass-whipping to dish out."

No one laughed.

"What about going straight? One of them went straight," Dave said.

"Perimeter first," Vitale said.

"Sir, how many people were here? I mean, overall," I said.

"Keel has more intel than I'd been given, but he said seventy-ish. Around fifty residents. Medical and military personnel were at twenty. Makes it some seventy people here. We stick to the plan. Marf, west. We're going east." Vitale waved his arm. Chatterton and Spade followed.

"We stay close," Marf said. "I'll take point. Dave, and then Chase, you be the eyes in the back of our heads. We're not going to go fast. We're going to stay close to the fence. Walk along it."

"Didn't we just do that, but from on the other side?" Dave said.

"We did and we're doing it again. This time, we are looking around the actual compound. Out there, we weren't focused on the inside. Only on getting to the gate," he said.

Again, we crouched, moved along the fence.

The apartments looked crudely constructed with wood frames and a few windows. Then the clouds passed over the moon. Darkness fell over us like a blanket being dropped over our heads. I couldn't even see my breath.

I saw a beam of light. Marf must have had a flashlight. Of course he did. These guys were better than boy scouts were. Trained to be prepared. It worked for him, up in front. Back here, all I could see was the thin beam of white light. He kept it aimed down. The light was like a laser, precise and contained. It wouldn't necessarily attract unwanted attention.

I kept looking behind me.

Might not be able to see my breath, but I could sure as shit hear my breathing. It was fast and heavy. I couldn't figure out how we would be able to find much of anything in such complete darkness. I assumed Marf used his small light to follow the tracks. Aside from the tracks, we had nothing else to go on.

If there wasn't Marf's light and the fence to assist, I'd be lost and stumbling blind. It already felt like a dream, a nightmare, with my feet sticking in the mud, the darkness and the sense that I'd never get where we needed to go. If I start hearing *chh-chh-chh-ha-ha-ha*, I would not be surprised, because part of me expected it. My imagination flared and it was getting the better of me. I'd wanted to help find the lost soldiers, but couldn't help regretting it now. I wanted to be back on the boat, back with my kids and Allison. I might be surrounded by the military, but I no longer felt safe. They knew little more than I did. Only real difference was training and weapons. They had them; I did not.

The clouds passed. The moon was out.

There was a building just to our left. It was set out from the rest of the apartments. I tried to remember the layout that had been explained. Thinking it is the military barracks. Place where the soldiers on site slept.

I saw Marf's fist shoot up, so we stopped. I looked left, right and behind us. The silence unnerved me. I didn't hear crickets. Nothing. I couldn't hear the other group either. I wondered how they were doing.

Dave turned around. "We're going to clear the barracks."

"What about finishing the search of the perimeter?"

Dave shrugged.

Marf ran toward the wood steps that led to the front door. He waved us over.

"We're going in. Look around. Might be some extra weapons. We'll make a note of inventory, okay? Right now, we have enough to carry. We don't want to be weighed down, so we're just looking, but not taking stuff. Not now," Marf said.

"We're shooting though, right?" Dave said.

"We're not shooting unless we have to, understand?"

"I'm nervous," Dave said.

"It's okay. It's natural. If it makes you feel any better, I am, too. Very. My heart has gotta be going twice as fast as it should," Marf said. "We'll go on three. I'm going in first. Dave, you follow me. Chase, you stand guard. We can't risk all of us going in. Got it?"

We nodded.

Marf counted on his fingers. He climbed the three steps, and then reached for the door handle. It was a lever knob. He pushed down on it slowly.

Clouds floated over the moon, gradually becoming darker and darker. Dave went up the steps next. I put my back to the steps, leveled my weapon and swept it left and right. Fucking zombie wasn't sneaking up on me. No one was.

Darkness consumed everything once again.

I heard the door open. The latch releasing sounded like an M-80 exploding.

Gunshots rang out.

"What the fuck was that?" Dave said.

I dropped to a knee and aimed my weapon toward the sound to the right. No, it had come from the left. Son of a bitch if I could tell from where it came.

"Chase?" Dave said.

"I don't see anything. Nothing," I said. I think I was whispering. Felt as if I yelled. I couldn't tell.

The next shots came from inside the barracks behind me.

"Chase!" Dave said. No doubt, he'd yelled.

I got up, spun around, leapt up and passed all three steps.

"One down," Marf said. "I got one."

He used his flashlight to play it over the room. There were no walls. Roughly ten cots. Footlockers. Two doors at the opposite end of the boxy room.

Someone was dead. The body was splayed in the middle of the room on the slatted wood floors. Marf went down, shining his light under the beds. "Chase, you're supposed to be outside."

"I heard the shots," I said.

"I fired once," he said. "That first shot was from the other side of the camp. Must be Vitale's group."

"Should we go help them?" Dave said.

"We won't. And they heard our shot and won't be coming to help us, either," he said. He got to his feet, approached the dead person.

The body was face down. The back of the head displayed a large hole. Brain matter and blood flowed down the neck. Not a good sign. Not good at all.

"He's bleeding," Dave said.

"Shit," Marf said. "He came right at me."

Using a foot, Marf rolled the person over. The bullet hole was squarely centered on the guy's forehead. Could be military. The crew cut was hint, if you ask me. It was too dark to see the clothing. Marf only shone the light on the guy's head. I didn't see dark black veins, and although his eyes were closed, I suspected he hadn't been a zombie.

"Shit," Marf said again. He knelt by the body, pulled dog tags out from under the white t-shirt. He held them in his palm and looked at them for a long time. "Soldier must have been hiding. Heard us come in."

"Why wouldn't he be hidden and just shoot at you, or something," Dave said. "I mean, why *come* at you?"

"Why come at me," Marf said out loud. He tucked the dog tags into his breast pocket and leaned forward. He used a thumb and finger to part one of the closed eyelids with his light a foot from the dead guy's face.

"Awe, shit," Marf said.

The milky eyes confirmed it. Zombie. Walking dead military guy. Marf hadn't killed someone hiding, waiting to be rescued. He'd taken out a monster. "Must have recently turned," I said.

"Must have." Marf stood. "You two, go back out front. Watch the door. I'm going to check the back rooms."

I wanted out of the barracks anyway, so I left. Dave was on my heels. We went down the steps. "Check that side of the building. I'll check by the other, and along the fence."

"I really can't see anything out here," he said.

"Just check," I said.

The gunshots had to have been heard back at the boat. I didn't want my kids scared. I didn't want them worrying that something bad might have happened to their father. Allison had them; she'd comfort them.

I looked along the fence best I could. Maybe four feet between it and the barracks. Nothing seemed to be moving. Not toward me, not in the opposite direction. Pretty sure it was clear.

"Nothing," Dave said.

I jumped. "You scared the fuck out of me."

"Sorry. Nothing on my side," he said.

"Same here. Think we're okay."

Marf came out of the barracks. He stood on the top step. "This one's empty. Now," he said, "let's finish this perimeter check."

More gunshots echoed off the nothingness of the ghost camp. They came from everywhere. Then stopped. More followed. I heard someone yelling. Could not identify the voice. Not even if it was male or female.

"I wanna say fuck the perimeter," Marf said. "That ain't just a shot to put down a zombie. They're fighting."

"So let's go," Dave said.

It was so dark. I didn't want to run, stumbling through the camp. There were too many structures to run past. Anything could be behind any one of them.

"Same as before. Stay close. Follow me," Marf said.

We didn't run, but we moved fast, staying low and close.

Thoughts passed through my mind. I hated them, but there was no way to shut it off. I wish I could.

Some seventy people had been here at the camp. Place looked deserted. Wasn't, obviously, but I'd be shocked to find seventy people here. Gates were open when we arrived. Something could have gotten in. Spread the infection. More than likely, the infection was already here. People gradually turned until the scales tipped. It probably happened fast.

The gates were open.

Uninfected might have escaped. I'd wager many had and were probably off hiding in the woods around the state park. Maybe they snatched boats from slips at the dock. When we pulled up, I don't recall seeing a single one there.

The diseased might have escaped, as well and then went after the uninfected. They might have fled to the woods and they were out there in the park hunting for food right now.

The Coast Guard personnel were armed. Despite a direct order to kill Captain Keel, Spencer stood guard like a centurion.

It would be foolish to think there weren't zombies in the area. I never disillusioned myself that way. The idea of seventy zombies roaming beyond the fence seemed worse for my family, more dangerous even than my searching within.

I wanted to get back to the ship. Needed to.

"Keep up," Dave said.

"I'm right behind you," I said. I was close. In fact, I was practically up his ass, as my father used to say.

We passed apartment buildings. They perfectly lined either side. After four sets, we stopped. Marf stood and pressed his back against one building. Dave and I followed suit.

"Main yard is over there. I see one large structure. Should be two smaller ones on either side and just in front of the main one," he said.

"What are they?" Dave said.

"The big one is the M.A.S.H. facility used for medical testing, sick bay, and that kind of thing. Mess halls will be the other two. And if I saw it right, the stage is on our side," he said.

There hadn't been a single gunshot or scream since we'd started running toward the sounds.

Marf used the radio. Talked into his sleeve. "Sergeant? Sergeant?" I heard his voice in the bud in my ear.

"Go ahead, Lieutenant. Over."

"The shots. You guys okay? Over."

"Back barracks. Came in to find a handful of zombies. Fast ones. Got the drop on us, so to speak. Chatterton got hurt. Not bit. We're okay. Over."

"Shit," Marf said. It wasn't into the radio. "We're going to have to get back to our spot." He held his cuff up to his mouth. "Okay, sir. Over and out."

We started back the way we had come.

We moved slowly, checking around corners.

Fast zombies were locked away in one of the military barracks. That was a good sign. Someone had to have lured them in and locked them inside. Vitale had disposed of them. Nice.

The moan came from behind me. Loud. Low. A grumble into an agonizing cry.

"Down," Marf said.

I dropped and splattered into mud.

Heard a gunshot.

"Get up, get up," Marf said.

I tried, but my shoes had no traction at all. They were coated in shit. My feet kicked and kicked, as if I was running in place.

Dave grabbed my shoulders and pulled me up. I turned around. The zombie was down.

He had not been alone. I saw heads bouncing. Couldn't count them, but there were more than three. They were coming and they were coming fast.

Marf took another shot. Then another. "Go, run. Go!"

# CHAPTER THIRTEEN

*Sunday, November 1st -- 0212 hours*

The dark was complete with the only light coming from the front end of Marf's gun when he fired off rounds. I had not fired a shot. I held my rifle with both hands across my chest. Running was difficult, but I gave it my all. I slipped, slid, and felt like I wasn't getting anywhere. Dress shoes sucked. I wished I'd changed out of them when I'd had the chance, back when I'd met my kids at my apartment -- long before the military Humvee rescued us from off the roof of the sidewalk plaza. I hadn't, so now, I was stuck with fucking shitty shoes caked in crappy mud.

The good thing? Zombies hadn't caught me. While I wasn't looking back, I figured they couldn't be doing much better in the mush. Fast zombies or not.

They groaned and grunted. The sounds forced chills racing up and down my skin, as if a skeletal finger made of ice traced my spine. I anticipated fingernails scraping my back. Each step I made was hopefully a step closer to getting away.

Dave and I ran side-by-side. His heavy breathing assured me I wasn't alone. Once, maybe twice, when I stumbled, he grabbed my arm like he could see just fine in the darkness. I felt muscles tense each time he snatched me up, startled, sure it wasn't him, but a zombie about to bring me down.

"Left!" Marf shouted.

We reached the end of the apartment. I think the fence was ahead. The gate to get out would have been to the right -- more back toward the way we had just run from, but to the right. Left only threw us deeper into the camp.

There was no time to argue. I went left, Dave now behind me. Losing my footing, I went down, and face planted into mud. I crunched my fingers against the butt of the gun when I fell on it. Dirty, cold and about to be eaten.

Dave, at least I think it was Dave, had hands on me. I felt the back of my pants and shirt pulled on.

I was lifted several inches, and then dropped back into the mud. I let out an *Ooomph!*

Something hit Dave hard, tackling him to the ground. They fought. Dave struggled, throwing wild punches from under the monster.

I attempted rolling over by using the rifle for leverage. I pushed on it, but before I could turn, a body slammed into me and onto me. The rifle flew out of my grasp. No chance holding onto it, because it was like my hands were slicked up with Vaseline.

The thing growled, hissed and its black tongue darted out of its mouth, licking at air, as if it wanted to clean the mud off my face. Putrid breath assaulted my nostrils. Acrid, and bile smelling, rotted flesh, like it decayed internally and the rancid fumes escaped from its mouth in plumes like smoke from a chimney.

Its jaws snapped at my face. I braced my forearm against its throat.

Clouds floated past the moon. That light was like a halo and outlined the zombie's head. Perfectly encircled it. It illuminated dark veins in its skin that streaked from the neck toward the eyes. Most of its right cheek had peeled back from the face, leaving gums and teeth exposed, and flapping as he snapped at me.

Another zombie tried to stop. Its feet kicked up mud, resembling a cartoon character about to take off sprinting. Flintstones is what I thought of. The crazy things that came to mind when I was in trouble made no sense. The thing fell to its knees between Dave and me. It had its pick and could make a dog pile out of either one of us.

I heard several gunshots, but didn't see muzzle flashes. Expected one of the zombies Dave and I fought against to drop, waited for brain chunks to rain down. Knew Marf was an excellent shot. The zombie on me, nothing. If he'd been shot, he didn't show signs of it. His teeth nearly rattled loose each time he snapped at me and only snagged at bites of air.

The third zombie dropped onto me over my head. I gasped. Claustrophobia kicked in. I bucked, and arched my back. My forearm still restrained the one at my throat. The second kept trying to get an angle that would allow him access to my face. My rifle was way out of reach.

I had a knife with a giant blade on my hip. With my free hand, I reached for it, thinking for sure it wouldn't be there, and the sheath would be empty, but it wasn't. My muddy fingers wrapped around the hilt. I yanked it free. I brought it up and plunged it into the first zombie's temple. The blade was sharp. It cut through the soft tissue and sawed clean into the brain. He fell forward, over me. Working like a shield, he protected me from the second zombie.

I tugged on the blade, but could not get a tight grip, because my hand kept slipping off. Using both hands, I pushed on his chest and rolled out from under him. The second zombie wasn't fooled. He scrambled up over the dead one; the one with my knife lodged in his brain. My rifle was just out of reach. I clawed my fingers into the mud, dragging myself toward it.

Hands locked onto my leg, so I kicked my free leg at its arm, trying to pry it loose. The muddy shoes weren't hurting shit, weren't delivering any *kick* in the kick.

The rifle was right there. I could see it, but I just couldn't get to it, despite the effort.

I sat up, balled my hand into a fist, and threw an uppercut at its jaw. Its head fell back, bounced forward. Its milky eyes rolled, *I think*. It screeched like metal being ground against a spinning stone. I would have plugged my ears if I didn't need to get the creature off my leg.

I pulled up my knee and drove the flat of my muddy foot into its nose. Heard bone crunch. Dripping mud revealed a flattened snout and missing front teeth. That would certainly help, but I didn't trust the lack of front choppers to save me.

The kick to its face might not have knocked him out cold the way it would have a real person. The hand did release my leg. I backed away, spun around and dove for the rifle. Falling on my back was the best I could do.

The thing was on all fours crawling at me. It was more wolf-like than we had been when we first rounded the enclosed camp. Its breath huffed from its mouth. Its head was low and it growled like a beast about to strike down prey.

I wrestled with the rifle, finger on the trigger and pulled.

White flames danced from the front of the muzzle. Six shots. Bullets tore its head to shreds.

Dave!

I got to my knees, ready to help my friend.

Dave straddled the zombie's chest and, was in the process of destroying its face with hammering blows from the butt of his rifle.

No doubt in my mind that my shots would attract more zombies. I was winded. Lungs burned. Cold tears streaked the mud as they rolled down my face. "We have to find Marf," I said.

"You okay?"

"I am. Killed two. Not like you. Only fighting off one."

"Go fuck yourself," Dave said, and smiled.

# CHAPTER FOURTEEN

*0247 hours*

"Where's the Lieutenant?" Dave said.

We stood with our backs pressed against one of the apartment buildings, both of us trying to control labored breathing. It began to rain again. The air was more than crisp. In fact, it was downright frigid. Temperatures seemed to keep dropping. Wet and muddy, I was cold. "I didn't see. No idea where he went," I said.

"This is kinda out of control now," he said. "I mean, we came looking for three soldiers. I was down with that. It made sense to me. They helped us, so in good conscience, I couldn't leave them out here. Not if there was a chance to save them."

"I agree," I said.

"But not now, I mean, now it's all different. You know what this is, don't you? It's a war. More than a battle. We're at war," he said. It was the most I'd ever heard him talk. Ever.

"We can't leave them," I said.

"I never said that," he said.

Maybe we were all thinking it, though.

He pointed at me. "You, too?"

I nodded. "I just want to get back to the ship and be with my family. It's all I've ever wanted, but I can't just leave, just go back there. There was a time I think I could have, but not now. We have to try to find them," I said.

"Some of them."

I agreed, "Some of them"

Hated to think I mostly figured on *just* Lieutenant Marf. Not sure I was up to going after Vitale's group. They had the two soldiers and Chatterton with them. They could fend for themselves, as we were. While I hoped to find and help Barron, Palmeri and Saylor, I think my faith that they were still alive was shaken, if not completely shattered.

Gunshots brought me out of my train of thought. "Where'd that come from?" I said.

"Behind us. All I can tell. Behind us."

One at a time, I wiped my palms down my pants, but it did nothing, because there was as much mud and moisture on them as there had been on my hands. There was nowhere to clean them off. All I could imagine was dropping my rifle again. That was my lifeline and I didn't want to risk losing it. I would have to do my best, and hope for it. The best. "Okay. Follow me," I said.

I must be losing my mind, because I'd just volunteered to take point. No idea what I was thinking, just that I couldn't be thinking straight. Point was a good way to go and get myself killed. Dead was the last thing I needed right now. Dead or worse.

"Right behind you," he said.

The moon glow was about the only Godsend I'd witnessed since finding my kids. How pathetic have my last several days been? I silently counted to three, pushed off from the structure frame, and ran around the corner.

Something exploded.

A ball of fiery light shot into the sky. Flames mixed with black smoke. The heat reached where we stopped. I thought my eyebrows singed.

"Son of a bitch," Dave said. "What do you think that was?"

It came from the center of the camp, I thought, but I couldn't be sure. Question now, do we head toward or away from the fire? Toward could be a death sentence. The explosion would attract zombies. Noise did that. The fire might harm them. It would be awesome if the explosion killed most of them.

"I think we need to get back to the ship," Dave said.

I couldn't disagree.

Someone screamed. The person was crying out was clearly in pain. It could be that he was being eaten alive, or had been injured by the explosion.

Shots were fired behind us from outside the camp. Who was outside the camp? Spencer. That was who. Spencer who accepted orders to shoot Travis Keel if the fucker tried to pull the Coast Guard vessel away from the slip.

Was the good Captain hightailing it? Leaving with my kids? This sucked. It sucked because if he did pull the boat away, I'd be thankful. My family would be safer on the water. Those things weren't going to swim out and attack the boat. That meant I had time to see who was screaming for help, and the truth was I really didn't want to.

We didn't run. We cautiously slinked toward the fire. Definitely, something burned toward the center of the camp. The sound was amazing. Loud. Crackling. Popping. Wet wood was defenseless against heat this intense. I smelled a combination of things burning. Some of it had to be flesh. Cooking flesh.

"It's where the zombies are going, too, you know," Dave said.

I put my sleeve to my mouth. "Lieutenant Marfione? Sergeant Vitale? Anyone?"

I stopped walking, waited and hoped for a response. Dave was right. The explosion had been loud. The noise would work like a bug zapper with flies. Attract them, but not necessarily kill them unless they curiously walked right into the flames. I'd seen them fall off a bridge into a river to get to us. It wasn't that far-fetched to think they might walk right into the fire.

"You think Vitale or someone blew something up on purpose? You know, get them all to one spot?" he said.

It made sense. A lot of sense. Sounded like a military maneuver. A hunter's scheme. A bait-n-shoot. The zombies were the deer.

"Marfione? Vitale?"

"Marfione here, over." It was a whisper. Barely heard it. I pressed a finger against the bud and tried pushing it deeper into my ear, but the transmission ended.

"It's McKinney, sir. We're trying to find you," I said.

"What exploded?" Marf said. "Over."

"No clue, sir. Where are you? Are you okay?" I wasn't saying the 'over' shit. When I was done talking, he'd know it. Then he could talk. It wasn't that complicated.

"In one of the apartments. They came from behind me. We were getting sandwiched. How are you, how's Rivera?"

"We're good. We're fine. We want to find you."

"Won't be hard. I'm in the apartment with the zombies outside of it. I can see them through the window. They're everywhere. Thought if I were quiet they'd get bored and leave, but that hasn't happened."

I looked left and then right. Dave and I had not gone far. We, from what I remember, rounded one corner. The very next corner might be as far as Marfione got. Figured that had been the one Marf had gone around, as well. I didn't see any zombies outside one of the apartments. I raised an eyebrow at Dave.

"I don't see any," he said, with a finger pressing his bud hard against his ear, too.

I hadn't heard anything from Vitale, Spade, or Chatterton. "You sit tight, Marf. We're coming for you."

"We are?" Dave said.

I knew what he thought. He was a brave man. He had Sues now. Without his brother, she was all he had. Like me wanting to get back to Allison and my kids, he wanted to get back to her. The more time we spent out here, the less likely it was we'd ever return. I knew it. He must, as well.

"We're getting him fast and then we're out of here."

"So we're looking for a swarm of zombies. First time we've hunted them," he said, and laughed.

I put a finger to my lips. "Shhh, are you kidding me?"

"Sorry. It's just, Chase, we're looking for a bunch of zombies."

I got it. Didn't like it, but I got it. The fire was not going out but seemed to grow. Red flames licked and roared at a black sky. Wonder if other structures caught fire, too? Think the rain might prevent a fire from spreading at least. Everything *was* so damned wet.

"Let's find a swarm of zombies and get out of here," I said.

# CHAPTER FIFTEEN

*0308 hours*

They knew he was inside. No way could they smell him. The ones that chased him into the apartment before he slammed the door must have started scraping the wood, and tapping fingernails on the glass window. Then there was the moaning. Growling. Maybe it was like a call that told other zombies they had trapped a potential meal. Combined, it was more noise than I would of thought possible without an actual word being said. The ten, twelve of them there were all doing it, scratching, tapping and moaning. Growling. Yeah. Oh yeah, it was loud enough to attract the attention of *more* zombies to the area.

I'd also have guessed that the explosion would call some away. Didn't seem to be the case. The food was here and they were intent on waiting it out, or scratching a way through the wall to get inside. Giving up didn't seem like it belonged in their vocabulary, but they didn't speak, so vocabulary was not accurate. Not at all.

"That's a lot," Dave said.

I hated that most of them wore military uniforms. Some carried rifles strapped around their shoulders and slung over their backs. Doubted they knew how to use them, fire back at us. Hell, they couldn't even figure out how to open the door.

I took a knee.

"You a good shot?" Dave said.

"Don't think I have to be. From here, we can just shoot into the group."

"If they're fast ones, they'll come at us."

I bit my upper lip. "The two of us shooting, I think we got it."

"Think?"

"Got a better idea? Want to go in closer. Hand-to-hand?"

Dave raised his rifle, closed one eye. "Monkeys in a barrel."

Think it's fish. Not monkeys. The kids' toy was those looped arm plastic red monkeys. They came in a barrel. Didn't matter, was neither here nor there. I took aim, as well.

"If they charge, might be easier to shoot. They'll be closer. Bigger target," Dave said. "And right in front of us."

Before I could answer, he opened fire. My ears rang. My head buzzed. Not wanting to be outdone, rather being told to *Go Fuck Myself*, I pulled the trigger.

They weren't monkeys, and they sure as shit aren't fish. A cluster of zombies, and us maybe twenty yards away, we shouldn't have missed as many as we did. Should have been a lot easier. The moonlight, the fire, it helped, but not enough, apparently. We sucked. The darkness, which was still too consuming made seeing difficult and accuracy nearly impossible. For us, anyway.

I hit one though. Was my bullet for sure. Took him in the gut. Watched thick blood spray. He went down. I thought, fuck headshots!

No sooner had I thought it, the mother got slowly onto all fours. Pushed his way up, and stood. I swear that fucker looked right at me, as if it knew I was the one that shot him. He spit out a mouthful of gunk. The bulk splatted into the mud. The rest dangled on a thick string of goo from his lower lip. When he charged, I panicked.

My hands fumbled on the rifle, needlessly. I felt my fingers loosen, grip, and then I brought the weapon up and aimed it as best I could before firing.

However, I hit nothing. Fired again. Nothing. It wasn't my fault. Blame the mud. The thing did lose its balance, slid, but didn't fall. My bullet must have just missed, whizzed by his head. That was my guess. What I was sticking to.

"Dave," I said. A heads-up to the fact that the thing was headed right for us fast. The camouflage it wore didn't hide shit. It looked like a brick house running straight for me.

I opened both eyes, blinked, and saw it correctly. Behind my giant soldier were the rest of the zombies. They must have realized they couldn't open a fucking door to get at Marf, and that Dave and I couldn't hit shit, so screw it, they'd follow the leader. And their leader was headed right at us.

"Run," Dave said.

Run where, I thought. I didn't want to get separated. "Into an apartment," I said.

"What about Marfione?"

"He is on his own right now," I said. "Now run."

Getting up from kneeling, my foot slid. I used the butt of the rifle as a cane, pushing up, got to my feet and ran.

Dave fired off another shot. "I'm behind you."

Behind me. Great. Where was I headed?

The next apartment was closer to the center and closer to the fire. Last thing I wanted was getting inside and then burning to death. I grabbed the door handle. The door opened and I dove in.

Dave's word was true. He was right behind me.

The door was closing slowly. Too slowly.

"Close it," I said. I couldn't move. Dave was on top of me.

He skidded off. The mud made any traction difficult. We both kicked around. Dave crawled on his belly toward the door.

One of the zombies was at the entrance before we could shut the door.

"Shit," I said. I wrestled with the rifle. The strap. Holding it correctly.

It walked up the last step.

"Chase!" Dave said. He could not get up. The wood floor was streaked as if covered in oil.

The zombie was missing most of its face. Clearly, something had bitten off its cheek. The exposed blackened gums and rotting teeth were all I saw when it opened its mouth. It stepped into the apartment, just as I got to my knees.

"Down!"

It wasn't Dave.

I dropped, regardless. I held onto my rifle, but dropped with my belly flat on the floor.

A gunshot rang out. A hole instantaneously appeared in the center of the thing's forehead. It stood there.

Dave kicked it in the chest.

It fell backward, down the two steps and splattered into a pool of mud. Dave did not waste time. He fumbled for the door, pulled it closed and locked it.

"Holy fuck," he said.

I panted and looked around. The apartment was dark. Far too filled with shadows, despite the windows and fire outside, to see who else was inside.

"Hello?" I said.

"Were either of you bitten?" A female voice asked.

"Who is there?" I said.

I heard a shotgun pump. "Were either of you bitten?"

"No," Dave said. "No, neither of us was bitten."

Silence. I tried to see in the darkness, to no avail.

"Hello," I said, when I could take the silence no longer.

"Who are you?" the woman asked. That wasn't quite fair, since I'd asked first. I deserved an answer first. Whoever she was, she had the advantage. Her eyes must be adjusted to the lack of light and she had a weapon obviously aimed at us.

"I'm Chase and that's Dave. We came over with the Coast Guard and just got here, maybe an hour ago, but I'm not sure. Wasn't long ago, though." My hands were out, reaching, fingers stretching, looking to touch something. Anything.

"Stay still," she said. "Who was the captain on the boat?"

"Keel," Dave said. "Travis Keel."

# CHAPTER SIXTEEN

*0410 hours*

The four of us sat with backs to the wall.

"They got Barron," Private Elysia Palmeri said. Her knees were up, her rifle standing between her thighs. Her hands gripped the barrel. It seemed like an actual part of her body. With ripped sleeves and dried mud covering her face, I could only imagine the battle that unfolded.

Private Christopher Saylor's ankle was wrapped in a crude splint. Wood stakes were tied in place with torn bed sheets. I had no idea where his boot was. I didn't see a rifle. He held his sidearm, his finger just outside the trigger guard. His elbows rested on drawn knees, head down.

"He okay?" Dave said, as if Saylor wasn't even in the room.

Palmeri looked at her partner and then Dave, nodding slightly. "We rounded a corner. Nothing, right? So we moved forward. Figured the place was deserted. Hoped it was, you know? As we made our way toward the center of the camp, we could see the M.A.S.H. unit, the mess halls, and not one fucking zombie. Then Barron, who was behind us, screams. Not like he's hurt, but like he's surprised as fucking hell. Caught off guard. We both turned around, and saw two of them had him down. He lost his footing. Must have been easy pulling him onto his back. He screamed as he punched and kicked at the two that attacked him. Saylor was trying to get a shot off, but it was so dark. They were bucking and squirming around. There was no shot. And the whole time Barron's screaming. Like a fucking pansy. He's just howling. 'Get them off me, get them off me.'"

We'd heard the screaming all the way at the boat, coming over the radio. He sounded as if he had been getting ripped apart. Shredded limb from limb.

"I told the sergeant. Said that Barron was down, you know? Don't know what I expected. Truth is," she closed her eyes, "I kind of panicked. Saylor couldn't get a shot off, and those things were just freaking creepy. I can't blame Barron. It was like he was covered with spiders. I hate spiders. God, I hate spiders. As much as I suffer from arachnophobia, these things are worse. No shit, right? So I don't know. My training kicked in. I used my rifle and started smashing it into skulls. Swinging this bastard like an ax." Palmeri lifts her rifle and drops the butt onto the wood floor. It tap-tap-taps.

"I shot one," Saylor said. First word since Dave and I made it inside the apartment. "I shot one, but I shot Barron, too."

"It wasn't a fatal shot for Barron, anyway." Palmeri put one hand on Saylor's shoulder. "It was a good shot. The way they were moving around, it was a very good shot."

"Barron never stopped screaming. That thing got him. Bit him. Had pieces of Barron's throat in his teeth. Blood gushed from Barron's neck. Squirted." Saylor sat with his back to the wall. He looked to the ceiling. I couldn't see if his eyes were open. I couldn't tell if he was crying. "I shot that thing again. In the skull. His brains blew out the back of his head. He fell over, dead for real this time. Dead for good." Barron had been bitten.

"And Barron?" I said.

Palmeri shook her head. "I did it. We didn't want him to turn. He knew. He was dying anyway. Losing blood. Losing so much blood. There was nothing we could do for him."

"There was nothing anyone could have done." Saylor got to his feet. He coddled his left leg, hand covering his knee. He limped away from the wall toward one of the beds.

"Don't let them see you," Palmeri said.

"They aren't tall enough to see inside the windows," he said.

"McKinney?"

I pressed the bud in my ear and spoke into my sleeve. "Marfione?"

"Where are you guys?"

"Is that Lou?" Palmeri said.

"It's Marfione," I said.

Palmeri pulled the bud from my ear and put it into hers. She talked into the radio on her sleeve. "Lieutenant, Lou? It's Palmeri, sir."

I was out now and couldn't hear the conversation. Dave listened. Saylor wasn't. Somehow, he and Palmeri must have lost their buds during the struggle and fight. It must have been pulled out, ripped off.

I waited, tried to listen, but heard nothing. Finally, Palmeri pulled the bud out of her ear; it dangled from my shoulder. I picked it up and plugged it back in. "Well?"

"Marf's okay. Holed up, like us. Says he's still surrounded. He's checking floorboards. See if he can't crawl out, sneak away," she said.

"And us?" I said. "What's our plan?"

I was only too happy to turn over command. Dave looked to me for leadership. That was fine when it was the two of us, but it wasn't a burden I wanted. With Palmeri and Saylor, I could relinquish it back to the military.

Then I looked over at Saylor.

One boot. A splint.

I thought about Chatterton when he was in the hull of his ship, talking to his people. The conversation I overheard when he thought I was asleep where he said my kids and I were a liability and was worried we'd slow them down.

I looked away. Looked at my own feet, for lack of anything else to look at. I felt ashamed. I thought the same way Chatterton had. I pursed my lips.

"What are you thinking?" Dave said.

I shook my head.

"You had an idea?" he said.

I shook my head again, just wanting him to drop it, and willing him to shut his mouth.

"I'll tell you what he was thinking," Saylor said. He was not using his inside voice.

Palmeri shushed him.

"No. Fuck that. I know what McKinney was thinking. I know what you're all thinking." He slapped his leg. "I'm going to get you all killed. I'm useless on the team."

"No one thinks that," Palmeri said. She lacked conviction in her words. She would be a terrible actress. "We're all getting out of here. Together."

My mind was a mess. I wanted to knock it around. The thoughts that filled it scared me. It wasn't me who was thinking such cowardly thoughts. Couldn't be. Survival of the fittest. Don't have to be the fastest, just faster than the slowest. Dammit! I needed the voices to stop.

"McKinney ain't thinkin' about me. He ain't worried 'bout us all getting back to the ship safely. Are you, Chase? It's just about you. Just about you and your kids, right?"

I held up my hands, palms out, shaking my head as if he had me all wrong.

"Well, fuck you," he said. "I got a family, too, you know. Kids. Two, just like you. But younger. Babies. In Maryland. Right outside D.C. Don't you think I want to be with them keeping them safe at home?"

I was silent.

"I'm with the fucking reserves. Got shipped here before all this shit broke out. Some training in the mountains. The Adirondacks. Was supposed to be just for a stupid weekend, and then they kept me here. My whole unit. They kept us here. Called my wife, told her. She was pissed. Never wanted me in the reserves anyway. This was icing on the cake for her, you know. Fucking something, she could throw in my face. I'd be missing my daughter's third birthday. My other daughter, my baby, wasn't even one yet. Yeah, that's right. Wasn't. Past tense. I haven't been able to reach them. I have no clue where they are, or if they're all right. Reports we got on the Capital," he stopped, head hung low. Web of one hand supported his forehead. "I'm not giving up. I'm finishing this mission, McKinney. I'm getting out of here and I'm done. I'm going home. I'm going to get my family. So fuck you. I'll go it alone if you don't want me slowing you down. I'll go it alone."

# CHAPTER SEVENTEEN

*Char kept Cash close and held his hand. It was kind of like before. Just different. Dad was off searching for missing people. The family was separated. What made it different was Allison. She was okay enough, but she wasn't Mom.*

*Mom. It was hard not to think about her. Wondering if she was all right? She couldn't be. She was one of them, a zombie, when she and Cash left the house. Had to leave, because Mom's husband attacked Char in the garage. He'd attacked her, and she'd chopped his hand off with an ax. It hadn't been safe to stay. Cash had been reluctant to leave. She convinced him that the only way they'd be safe was by finding Dad.*

*She'd been right. He'd been looking for them, too. She knew he would have been and that he would have come for them. That was Dad. Everything he did, it was for them. While Cash might be too young to realize it, she was old enough to see and appreciate it.*

*Like before, Dad would be back. She knew he would. In the meantime, there was no way she'd let go of her brother's hand. For what it was worth, Allison held onto her hand in pretty much the same way. Tight. Sweaty.*

*She hadn't grabbed for Cash's hand right away, and Allison hadn't held her hand until the explosion somewhere in the camp. The sound made everyone jump. There was a moment of silence; either that or her hearing had been impaired before the rolling ball of flames had been spat into the night sky.*

*That's when everyone held hands.*

*Three things happened, really. The explosion. The captain couldn't raise anyone on the radio. He tried, too. Kept shouting into the handheld and paced up and down. He looked like he depressed the button on the side so hard that his fingers might puncture plastic and wind up inside the thing. That was the second thing. The third was the one soldier standing like a guard by the ship.*

*That guy watched them. Seemed to watch everyone on the ship, especially the Captain. Thing was, the Captain kept watching the guard. Something was going on, and Charlene had no clue what. Nevertheless, when those three things happened, she snatched up her little brother's hand, and Allison snatched up hers.*

*The Coast Guard crew looked busy until the explosion. Once that rocked the night, they went from doing what looked like seamen things —reviewing maps, going up and down stairs, calling out to check for this and check for that—to staying positioned along the side of the boat with rifles.*

*The paramedic woman was with Crystal, the one from the other small group of survivors. The two talked, and whenever they caught Char looking at them, they smiled. It was one of those fake smiles, an everything-is-gonna-be-all-right smile. Unless they thought Char was four or dumb, then they were the oblivious ones. Clearly, nothing was going to be all right, or the same, or even halfway okay. And a stupid smile wouldn't make things any better. Whatever. She just pacified them with a returned smile that maybe showed off a few more teeth under a slightly curled lip than necessary, but so what.*

*"I don't have a good feeling," she'd said. She watched the flame ball roll into the sky. Maybe she'd reached for Allison's hand first. She definitely reached for Cash's.*

*"Is Daddy, okay?"*

*"He's fine." Char gave his hand a squeeze. "He's probably the one that blew whatever that is up. Killing zombies."*

*Cash smiled. "You think so?"*

"Think so? No. I know so," she said. "He's out there kicking zombie butt."

Cash giggled. "Yeah, he is."

"Yeah, he is," Char agreed.

She didn't believe it. She had no clue where her father was, if he was all right, or what caused the explosion and who was kicking whose butt.

The boat sat on the river with the only light coming from the fire. The flames did next to nothing to pierce the darkness that enveloped them.

"That's it," Captain Keel said. "We're done. We're pulling away."

"Sir?" the paramedic, Erway, said.

"We're pulling out. Not leaving, just going out onto the river. Not leaving, just getting away from land." Keel walked toward the helm.

Char tugged on Allison's shirt.

"Don't worry," Allison said. She let go of Char's hand. "Captain?"

"Not now," he said.

Char watched Allison rush toward the man. "Sir, we can't pull away. If they come back, if they're being chased, the boat needs to be here. They might not have time to wait for us to get back into the slip."

"It's what we're doing."

"I don't think..."

"Ms. Little, if you do not like it, if you have a problem with my command, you are more than welcome to get off my vessel and wait with Corporal Spencer," he said. "Deisenroth, fire up the engines."

"Sir," Allison said, grabbing the captain's arm.

He shrugged out of the hold with a violent shake. Allison stumbled backward. Erway caught her from behind.

Char watched Allison closely; knew she was working out what to do next. Had to be wondering whether they go or stay. Couldn't be an easy choice. Had to be made. "Allison," Char said.

*Allison nodded. Their eyes locked. "Don't let go of your brother."*

*"You're not seriously going to get off the vessel," Keel said.*

*"We are, and we're going to take some supplies. And these weapons." Allison spun around.*

*Keel reached out. His hands tugged on her hair. Erway stepped between them. "Captain!"*

*"You are not getting off the ship, and you most certainly are not taking anything that belongs the Coast Guard, ma'am." Fat fingers fumbled with straightening his tie clip. "Do we understand each other, Ms. Little?"*

*"I'm sorry. I do not believe we do." Allison backed away.*

*Char didn't need direction. She gathered their weapons, and from the footlocker, extra ammo and knives.*

*"Young lady," Keel said. "Maar, stop her. Stop that child."*

*Maar wore a Coast Guard baseball cap that clearly rested on a head of thinning hair. When he got close to Char, she dropped what she'd gathered. Dropped everything except the handgun. She brought it up, finger inside the trigger guard, arms extended with the barrel half a foot from Maar's forehead.*

*His hands went up. "Sir?"*

*"Ah, geez, Maar. It's a child."*

*"Don't matter how old I am, does it?" Char said softly, her words barely audible. "I could be six or sixty, and kill you the same. Isn't that right, Maar?"*

*He backed up.*

*"Cash, pick up the guns and the knives, now."*

*Allison and Cash picked up as much as they could. "This could have been avoided," she said.*

*"Here's the thing now, Ms. Little. You want off my ship, good. Go. Because when your friends return, when the military gets back, we'll bring them on board. But you and your kids, you're going to be stranded. Left here. Shit out of luck," Keel said.*

*Erway said, "Captain, I think we're…"*

*"Enough," Keel waved a hand at the paramedic. "Let them off the boat, Maar."*

*Like Maar had done anything to stop them.* Permission from the Captain didn't mean a thing, *Char thought.* I'd already granted myself permission.

*"Where are you going?"*

*Char took her eyes off Maar. Spencer was by the side of the boat. He was yelling. Deisenroth had revved the engines. In the silence of the night, they sounded like rockets firing up on the space shuttle.*

*"We're pulling out of the slip," Keel said.*

*"No. You're not. You want to keep the engines running, that's fine. But you, Captain, are not going anywhere," the corporal said.*

*"This is my ship."*

*"And I have my orders, Captain."*

*Travis Keel laughed. "What orders? I never gave you any orders."*

*"You're not my Captain, sir. I wouldn't take orders from you under any circumstances," Spencer said.*

*"These orders, what are they?"*

*"No reason I can't tell you. You try moving this boat; I put a bullet in your skull. I'm paraphrasing. Kind of. I think you get it though, don't you?" Spencer raised his rifle.*

*Maar looked sideways at Char. She cocked her head to the side. "No funny ideas," she said. She motioned with her gun for him to step aside.*

*She wanted her back to Spencer and the Coast Guard personnel in front. "Allison, you and Cash get off the ship."*

*"I don't think now's the time," Allison said.*

*"We're getting off," Char said. "Now."*

*"You must be out of your mind," Keel said. "You are not going to shoot a captain."*

*"I don't care if you were the president. You try to move this boat, and you're dead, and I'm not fooling around."*

*Char jumped. Didn't expect it. The gunshot boomed.*

*She stared at Keel. Thought he'd been hit. Way he put a hand to his chest, maybe he'd thought so, too.*

"Was a warning shot," Spencer said. "I've changed my mind. Shut the engine."

Keel removed his hand real slow. His lips spread wide and he laughed. "You are out of your mind, corporal. You know how many guns are aimed at you right now."

Char took a look around. All of them. Even Deisenroth with one hand on the wheel, one on a gun. Where were Allison and Cash? She didn't want to take her eyes off the Coast Guard. She never let her gun waver; if she pulled the trigger, Maar was dead.

Despite the engine chugging, the river water slapping up against the side of the ship, there was no mistaking two sounds. If the wind wasn't blowing, Char knew she'd smell them, as well.

Moaning.

Growling.

Both fast and sluggish zombies were coming.

She knew the sound attracted them. The engine. The warning shot. Calling cards. Zombies were coming. Getting off the boat didn't make sense.

Keel must have heard them, too. He wasn't laughing. His smile froze on his face. He looked up and to the left, but it was far too dark to see anything. He said something to Deisenroth, and then turned. "Get off my ship!"

Allison pushed Cash behind her. "The things are coming."

"You wanted off. You wanted to go wait for your man. Go. It's not a request. Get off my ship."

Spencer climbed aboard.

A gunshot was fired. Char didn't see who did it. She saw, instead, Spencer stumble back a step, another, hit the side of the boat before falling over and splashing into the icy river.

Something slammed into her arm. She dropped the handgun as she turned her attention back on Maar.

He twisted her arm at the wrist, spun her around and shoved her arm halfway up her back.

"Get them off my ship," Keel said.

"You can't do that," Allison said.

*"Break the girl's arm," Keel said.*

*Maar applied pressure. The threat, the possibility he'd break bone was very real. She didn't want to cry out, but couldn't hold it in. Pain shot through her arm to her shoulder. "Let go of me!"*

*Maar forced her to walk.*

*"Keel, tell him to stop," Allison said.*

*Keel shrugged. "We're pulling away. Either you get off right now, or once we pull away, we'll throw you into the water. All three of you."*

*"Captain," Erway said.*

*"Stop choosing the wrong sides, Erway. Learn your place, dammit!"*

*Erway grit her teeth and hefted a medical bag over her shoulder. "I'm getting off, too."*

*Again, Keel laughed. "You're not going anywhere. I've had enough."*

*The zombies were closer. Char couldn't tune them out. She couldn't look to see how many either. Cold tears filled her eyes. "Let me go, please," she said in a whisper.*

*"You put a gun to my head," Maar said. "Where was your mercy?"*

*"She's a kid. Leave her alone. She doesn't have a gun. She's not a threat."*

*The pressure stopped. Just like that. Gone. Char pulled her arm up to her chest and cradled it.*

*Allison was wide-eyed.*

*Char turned around. Maar wasn't behind her. He was balled up on the ground, out of it. Blood spilled from a crack on the back of his head.*

*Sues Melia held a fire extinguisher in both hands. She smiled. "Now what?"*

*The rest of the Coast Guard crew was on deck. Char counted them. Too many to fight. She bent down, picked up her handgun. "We're out of here," she said.*

*Allison said, "What?"*

*"We're not staying on the ship."*

"Charlene," Allison said.

Char faced her. "Staying on this ship isn't safe. They're crazy, Allison. We won't be safe. Look at him. The captain has lost his mind. They'll kill us. They just shot that corporal guy. See anyone flinch? We're getting off."

Char went to the side of the boat, put one leg over, and then the other. "Cash, come on."

Allison held her brother's hand.

Cash tugged and yanked in an attempt to pull free.

"She's right," Crystal said. She was on her feet, standing beside Sues. "I'm not staying."

"Come with us, Allison," Char said.

Keel fired three shots into the air. "Get off my boat. Now!"

"We were leaving. Why did you do that? Why did you fire that stupid gun? You just called more zombies over here!"

"Too fuck--"

Char shot him. She just raised her gun, pulled the trigger and shot the captain. The impact spun him around, arms flailing. He did more than a one-eighty, leaned over the helm, and swore as blood pooled and then spilled from the corner of his mouth.

"Oh, shit," Allison said.

Char was far from done. She aimed, fired and fired and fired.

The Coast Guard returned fire.

Screams came from everywhere. Char drowned out the noise. She concentrated instead on targets. And fired. And fired.

She only stopped when she thought she heard Allison scream out a name. Her ears rang from all the gunplay. A slight shake of her head would clear the clouding. That was when she heard it again. Only Allison wasn't screaming. Not anymore. Now she sobbed. Sobbed and said the same name, over and over.

"Cash. Cash!"

# CHAPTER EIGHTEEN

"I can walk," Saylor said. He shrugged off hands trying to help him. He held up his handgun. "I've got this."

He could walk. He'd never be able to run. He winced every time he put any weight on his leg. Ankle was probably worse than a sprain.

"We going for Marf?" I said.

"See if he's out." Palmeri checked the clip in her rifle. Seemingly satisfied, she locked it back in place.

"Marf?" I said into the radio.

"Yeah," he said. No 'over' this time.

"You out?"

"No. Still here. Can't get out through the floors. Place is kind of well constructed, surprisingly, and if I'm not mistaken, there's even more zombies," he said into my ear.

I told Palmeri, and then went over the radio again. "Anyone else copy this transmission? Anyone?"

Silence.

Everyone looked at me. I shook my head.

The Coast Guard should hear us. They should be answering at the very least, but they weren't. I couldn't help wondering if we were going to return to an empty slip. The vessel gone. My kids, gone.

"Tell Lou we're coming for him."

It finally hit me. Lou, short for Lieutenant. I told him and he thanked us.

"You know where he is, right? You were at his apartment?" Palmeri said.

"About two back that way," Dave said, pointing. "I'll lead the way."

Palmeri nodded. "Okay. We go slow. I don't need to stress this, but we look in every direction all at once. Got it?"

We agreed.

Dave stood at the door with one hand on the knob. Saylor was by the window, silhouetted against the flames of the fire just beyond. He craned his head left and right.

"How do we look?" Palmeri said.

"Seven? Eight? I can't see everything, but they're out there."

As if to illustrate the point, something knocked against the door. Dave jumped back.

"They're milling around. They don't look like they're trying to get inside. Not really. They just look, I don't know, kinda lost," he said.

"Lost is good," Palmeri said. "We can surprise them, hopefully."

I took in a deep breath. Eyes closed. I saw the camp in my head, best I could remember it. The fence outlined everything. The apartments were in rows. We never made it past the center. Way it sounded, we never would. "I think we get Marf, and then we keep going west, toward the fence. Follow it around to the gate," I said.

"We should stay between apartments," Saylor said. Again, he spoke loudly, forgetting that his booming voice could attract unwanted attention. "We need to hide, get away from them, and the fence isn't going to help."

He might be right. "Okay," I said. "I agree."

"How lucky for me," Saylor said.

"Cool it," Palmeri said. She knew how to yell without raising her voice. "We're behind you, Dave. As soon as you're ready."

I exhaled.

"As ready as I can be," he said. He looked at me. I nodded. "Here we go."

I took a knee, raised my rifle and aimed.

Dave pushed open the door.

The door knocked two zombies over, sending them to the ground. Their arms and legs flailed; looked like they were making mud angels. I almost fired at nothing. Didn't have to wait long. Another creature stuck his head in the doorway. It was a woman who had long curly hair. Most of it was matted against her face, and neck. Her arms reached for us and we could see that her flesh was clearly bitten. Mouth-size chunks were missing up her forearm and the bone was exposed under what was left of her decaying meat and tendons.

I fired.

The bullet went through the bridge of her nose. Her eyes crossed as she fell forward. Dave kicked her body out of the doorway. He sent a few rounds into the mud angels. Their bodies danced as the bullets slammed into them, then nothing. They lay flat and still.

Three down, five to go, if Saylor had been correct. Five, if our gunshots didn't attract more.

"Move," Palmeri said.

Dave stepped out of the apartment. I was right behind him. I held my gun up, swiveled left and right. To the right were three more. I fired, missed, cursed, and fired again. *Chunked* out a slab of shoulder. The zombie jumped back, off balance, but didn't go down and didn't stop advancing. It slowed him, but nothing more.

I closed one eye and lined up the cross hair, ignored the sound of firing weapons, yelling and screaming around me. I fired again. Hit the eye. It popped in a spray of the black goo that once had been blood. Dropped it.

We were going to the left. The zombies were behind us, moving slowly. Steady, but slow.

I didn't want to take my eyes off them. I kept the rifle raised, but I didn't shoot. We were putting some distance between them. I kept an eye on Palmeri and Saylor.

I chanced a look around.

Dave was low, checking the corner before rounding it. He fired his rifle.

"Got a few over here," he said. "Shit. More than a few."

"Shoot 'em," I said. "Shoot them all!"

I hoped Saylor and Palmeri had our backs. I stood above Dave. We aimed at the zombies coming up the alley between apartment buildings and fired.

Two ran at us fast. They were decked out in military camo.

"Hit 'em, hit 'em," I said.

I was shooting. Headshots were tough, especially with them running. Heads bobbed. In shows and movies, the good guys hit everything. Destroyed brains like there was no way to miss. Crossbows sent arrows true. In real life, the here and now, it was different. So fucking different. The more apprehensive the situation made me, the harder it was to aim, but I kept firing.

And firing.

There was no other choice. None.

We nailed the fast ones. Might have been Dave or it could have been me. Like to think, it had been me. I gave up on keeping score. My ratio sucked anyway.

Suddenly, it didn't matter, anymore. I was out. No more clips on me. No ammo left. "I'm out, got nothing left!"

I held onto the rifle. It was my bat, my sledgehammer. It, and my knife, they were all I had to keep me alive.

"Get up!" It was Palmeri. I looked back and saw that Saylor had fallen and was face down in the mud.

I stopped.

Dave grabbed me by the shoulder. "Keep moving," he said.

I heard gunshots. Lots of gunshots. It wasn't us and didn't seem to be coming from the camp, so it had to be from the boat. I needed to get back to the boat. Dave was absolutely right; we needed to keep moving.

"Can you help me," Palmeri said. It was like she was crying out in desperation. I heard it in her voice. I shouldn't have done it, but I looked back a second time.

Palmeri kneeled next to Saylor. She had her handgun out. She used her free arm and snaked it under Saylor. He was not helpless, so he struggled to help her lift him.

"Dave," I said.

He fired at a zombie. "We keep moving."

I went back. Could not ignore the smell of the apartments burning. The raging fire kept getting closer. There was no worrying about the moon hiding behind clouds now. Flames lit the night sky better than the sun during most days. I dropped on the opposite side of Palmeri.

Dave ran at us. A spattering of flame burst from the front of the rifle barrel. I threw up an arm to shield my head. If Dave was shooting at me, my arm wasn't going to stop shit. It was just a reflex. Dave wasn't shooting at me. He was hitting, with pretty dead-on accuracy, the zombies coming at us from behind.

He reached us and dropped his rifle by my side. "I'm out, too!"

In a single, fluid motion, he had his knife out and was in the air. He slammed the heel of his shoes into a zombie's chest. The thing would have gotten me, no doubt. I hadn't seen it, or heard it, but it had been right behind me.

With a scream, Dave scrambled, spun around in the mud and threw his body across the creature. I stood up as Dave drove his blade into the zombie's throat. He tugged his knife across the flesh, sawing at the spine. He grabbed a fist of its hair and pulled on it as he snapped the head one way, the other, and back again until he was able to pull it free. He removed the whole head from the body and cast it aside.

Palmeri was up, too. She fired at the zombies coming from where we had been heading. She aimed and fired. Good shots. Dropped zombies like a pro.

However, we were stuck. With Saylor struggling to stand, we were trapped between two apartments with nowhere to escape to. We needed an out, and right now, I didn't see one.

I gripped the barrel of my rifle and swung at the head of a fast zombie. I knocked it off balance. It fell against the siding, clawing at the apartment to keep from hitting the ground. It knew it wanted to stay on its feet.

I raised the butt of the rifle and drove into the thing's face. Its head smashed. It looked like an overripe melon of some sort. The thing's nose was lost inside the skull and thick black blood oozed from where cheeks and teeth had been. It slumped to the mud, and then just sat there. Battered brains spilled from the huge orifice that was now the center of its face.

"We're surrounded," Dave said.

I looked left. Right. Wasn't quite surrounded. Sandwiched, yes. Sandwiched between the two buildings, and both possible ways out were filled with zombies. They were either slow or cautious. I preferred to think slow. Slow meant they weren't learning, weren't getting smarter, and were not afraid of us bashing in their brains.

Slow, or smart, didn't matter. We had nowhere to turn. Nowhere to go. "Dave," I said, holding up my knife.

The two of us could fight our way out.. Three, if Palmeri came. Saylor would be fucked though. No way to cut a safe path through with Saylor saddling down two of us. Just wouldn't work. Couldn't work.

Palmeri insisted on helping Saylor up. He stood with one arm out, as if reaching for a wall to support him. Palmeri slid under that arm. "I've got you," she said.

She didn't. He weighed twice as much as her. He'd bring her down. With the wet grass, the mud, no way they could run. Fucking zombies slow as turtles would be able to catch and eat them.

"Keep moving," Dave said.

I pursed my lips and tried to swallow. My throat felt dry, raw and my tongue swollen and thick. Sweat, rain, or mud slid down my forehead. Streaked my face. I wiped it with the back of my sleeve, and my sleeve onto the stomach of my shirt.

I didn't want to leave anyone behind.

Dave stared at me. He didn't say a word, but I saw it in his eyes. He screamed it with his eyes. *We keep moving.*

# CHAPTER NINETEEN

*0512 hours*

Our predicament resembled a mini-football field, and there were two teams involved; us versus Them. Felt like we were in the fourth quarter, at the two-minute warning. While I hoped we'd end this, worst case, I wanted to hang on long enough to go into overtime. It didn't look good. In fact, it looked down right terrible.

Two rectangular apartment buildings sat, one on our left, and the back end of an identical one to the right. To the west, behind us, six or seven zombies approached. Two wore simple hospital gowns with bare limbs exposed to the elements. If I had to guess, flaps were open in the back. Why I thought that, why that popped into my mind, I have no idea. Another wore unidentifiable clothing. It was burnt and melted to her body. Her face and arms had been blackened by heat and fire. If the hair around the charred face hadn't been so long, I'd never have known it was a woman. The others four were a mix of military and civilians. Men and women with bite marks evident and decay apparent. They were all obviously anxious to sink teeth into our flesh.

To the east, in front of us, there were another eight or so zombies. More gowns, more military, more civilians. My stomach rolled and flopped. I thought I might vomit and probably would.

I wanted a cigarette. A beer. A burger. I felt famished.

"Chase." Dave waved me on. He was ready. Time to go. Time to leave Palmeri and Saylor to their fate. She struggled to keep Saylor on his feet. His weight had to be wearing her out. He definitely rested it all on her shoulder.

A horrible fate.

I sucked in a deep breath and sprang into action.

Not toward Dave. I just couldn't. I ducked under Saylor's other arm.

"Get out of here," he said. "You guys have a better chance. Take Palmeri and get out of here. Fight a way through them."

"We're all getting out of here," I said. It couldn't be true and didn't even sound realistic when I said it out loud. Fairytale or not, I committed. "Now fucking help us, help us!"

Saylor's jaw tensed. He set his foot down, placed weight on his injured leg and winced. He manned up and hobbled with some speed.

Dave grunted, turned, and slashed his blade as if it was a Samurai sword with only an eight-inch reach. I didn't stop him. He ran into the converging mass. With a swipe, he sliced open a throat, drove the blade into an ear, and stuck it into a third zombie's Adam's apple.

"Chase, behind you," Dave said. He fought, killed, and was still able to warn me.

"Hold him," I said, not waiting for Palmeri to acknowledge.

I spun around. The burnt zombie closest to me had her arms out, and what was left of her mouth was open. The blackened skin peeled, flaking off her face. A black tongue darted out of her mouth, licking at air the way an iguana or snake might, as if blind, and it used that muscle to sense prey in the area.

With a slash, I chopped the tongue out of its mouth, and heard it plop into a puddle of mud. The thing stepped on its own tongue without losing a sluggish step toward me.

Grabbing it by the hair, I pulled the head forward and drove my foot into its gut. With it doubled over, I slammed my blade to the hilt into the back of its neck, and twisted.

Looking up, I saw more zombies coming. We were definitely surrounded. My breathing was quick and shallow.

Sweat dripped from my armpits. I felt claustrophobic. My eyes darted left and right, but I did not see a way out of this. No easy way.

I pulled out my knife. The zombie woman collapsed in a heap of dead carcass at my feet. I stepped around it to the side and used my elbow like a battering ram smashing it into the head of a hospital-gowned creature. Through a solid punch into the jaw of another, and used the blade to disconnect most of its head from the rest of its body.

I heard the others behind me, all engaged in a fight for survival.

One of those fast zombies charged from around a corner, knocking the slower shuffling dead from its path. I saw it, but could not react. My knife was buried deep into the flesh of a beast and I could not remove it. I let go of the handle and threw my hands up, which was the only way to defend myself from the attack.

A gunshot rang out.

In mid-flight, the fast zombie dropped, as if a bird shot out of the sky.

At the next set of apartments was someone with a rifle.

There was no time to yell out a thank you. I reached down, yanked my blade free and punched it between the eyes of the next gowned zombie. Holding the thing by an ear, I pulled my blade free, and the ear off of its head.

More shots came from whoever it was on the opposite side of the zombies. With deadly aim, he dropped creature after creature. He walked towards us as he fired. He used his rifle completely different from the way I had. I pressed the trigger like a person with an incurable twitch. He took single shots, hit a target, and then went on to the next.

I knew who it was, who it had to be. Not sure why, but I felt relieved.

As Spade got closer, the zombies around us got *more* dead.

I ran my shoulder into a zombie's back. It had turned from me and had been walking toward Spade. My knee crunched into its spine as we hit the ground. I ran the blade across the back of its neck, raised it high, and holding it in both hands brought it home. My hand shook as the sharp teeth on the steel chewed through its spinal cord.Spade held out a hand and pulled me up. "We're out of ammo," I said.

"I'm just about out, too."

There was no time, but I still wondered where Chatterton and Vitale were. Feared the worst. Got to a point where hoping for the best just didn't seem to make sense anymore.

Dave and Palmeri held their own. Spade and I joined their end of the fight. We ran past Saylor, who held his knife close to his chest. He must be out of ammunition as well. He appeared ready to battle anything that got close, and I'll bet thankful nothing had yet.

It resembled a barroom brawl. Punches thrown, kicks delivered. Dave head-butted a zombie, then crashed his elbow into the face of one behind him. Palmeri could scrap. She grabbed at arms, and broke bones with her knees. Thought I saw some martial arts training in her moves. Nothing Jackie Chan worthy, but by the speed and fluidity, it was evident.

The quicker we clear the dead the faster I could get back to my kids. With that in mind, that solitary inspiration, I kicked down at the top of a zombie's knee. The crunch of bone and cartilage was loud. The thing didn't cry out, but it crumbled. I stepped on its back. Pulled on its hair; ran the blade across its throat fast, hard, and again, before shoving the blade to the hilt through the temple. An eyeball popped from the socket, perhaps making room for the passing by of the blade's serrated edge.

Saylor screamed.

I looked up. He was down with two zombies on him. He stabbed at one of them repeatedly. The blade punctured the thing's side. Intestines spilled out. The zombie kept at him with mouth open and teeth bared.

The way Saylor's arm was almost pinned, there wasn't much more he could do. Without bullets to destroy the brains, simply slitting a throat or stabbing them repeatedly was as useless as blowing a hole in their chest with a shotgun. Had to stop the head, the brains, because all other efforts were pointless.

My feet fought for traction. The cold muddy ground was like ice. As I made my way toward him, I watched the second zombie, bite the lobe from Saylor's ear. It tore at the flabby flesh and tugged at it. The chewing is what disgusted me most. It gnashed teeth on Saylor's lobe, tongue licking at its lips to swipe at spilling blood.

Saylor screamed and screamed. Partly from the pain of the bite, I assumed, but mostly from anger. Angry he'd been bitten, and angry he couldn't do shit to get the zombies off him.

I dropped to a knee in front of it. The thing looked up at me, let out a guttural roar and hiss. I saw a small flab of lobe on its tongue, sloshing around inside its mouth. I stuck my blade into its mouth until the tip poked out of the back of its head.

The milky white eyes stared at me. No way had they seen me. Not anymore. I'd stabbed the fucking life out of it for good, for real, this time.

Saylor managed to kill the one he'd been struggling against, the one that had distracted him while the other ate his ear.

"It bit me, man. It bit me," he said. He was on one knee, the injured leg extended.

"You'll be all right," I said. No idea why. We both knew he was fucked.

He didn't even humor me; wasn't interested in being passive. He was military. He took action. What I never expected was the action taken.

He started to growl.

I thought, ah fuck, he's changing into one of them already? Was it that fast? How fucked was I being this close to him. I need to get up, get away, and keep moving.

I had been wrong. He wasn't changing. He was working up courage or strength, or both. All at once, he grabbed the top of his bitten ear with one hand and then with the knife in his other, severed the ear off. It wasn't a clean cut. It bled profusely. Blood just seemed to leak from the side of his head.

Saylor held his ear in front of his face. His jaw set, mouth open. Muscles bulged on his neck. His arms shot to his side. He looked up into the fiery night sky.

"I'm not going to turn into one of those things, McKinney. I fucking ain't, I just fucking ain't."

Spade came over and looked at the ear Saylor held in his hand. "It fuckin' bit you and you chopped your ear off?"

"Fuck yeah, I did." He was charged with energy with muscles tense all over his body.

"Fuck yeah!" Spade matched tempo. Had to be a military thing. Reminded me of a football team encircling each other on the sideline before the game, jumping up and down. Psyching each other up and out. Comrades. Buddies. Brothers.

They both howled. Except this time when Saylor looked to the sky like a wolf, Spade punched the heel of his hand into Saylor's face; drove the nose bone into the brain. Saylor fell over, flat onto his back. Mud splashed out around him.

"Can't risk it," Spade said. Not sure he was talking to me.

I stood up. Looked around. The carnage was everywhere. The dead finally dead and we'd lost one, which was too much. The guy had cut off his own ear to live. "Now what?"

"We get back to the ship; we get the fuck out of here."

"Lieutenant Marfione's holed up in one of these," I said. I used the radio on my sleeve. The bud dangled, resting on my chest. I lifted it and stuffed it back into my ear.

"Anything?"

"Nothing. But after the explosion we couldn't hear anyone earlier, just him, Just Marf." I tried reaching the L.T. again.

"The radios are crap. It's that simple. Government issue. The moisture, the distance – short as it is – could be a million reasons why it doesn't work. Ours, mine anyway, cut out right away."

Had Allison or my kids tried reaching me or tried to find out what was going on? Where or how we were doing?

We needed to find Marf, yes, but we needed to get back to the ship. I hadn't forgotten the shooting I'd heard earlier coming from their direction.

While I still wanted to know what happened to Vitale and Chatterton, I figured now was not the time. Guess I didn't need an explanation. It was kind of self-explanatory. Zombies were everywhere. Explosions. There was no need to ask. My imagination worked fine. They were dead. With Spade, I had no doubt, if they'd been bitten, they would not return as a zombie, either.

I yelled into my sleeve in one last attempt. "Marf!"

"I think it was the apartment back here," Dave said. "That one."

The one he pointed at could very well have been the apartment Marf was in. Had it of been, he would have seen us out the window. If he saw us from the window, why didn't he join the fight?

"Let's check," Spade said. He went forward and as he passed Palmeri, he hesitated long enough to touch her shoulder. Maybe there had been something between Palemeri and Saylor. More than I'd picked up on. I hadn't seen it but Spade's gesture revealed much, much more.

She didn't meet my eyes as I followed Spade. Silently, she fell in behind me. I heard the sloshing sound of her boots in the mud. I wished I could think of comforting words to share. Something I could say to ease her pain.

It was a new world. A different one. I got it. Gone were the days of comforting one another, if we ever really did that before. Pain was in surplus. Kind of like you didn't mind saying *God Bless You* when someone sneezed, but when the person lets out three or four in a row, you're like, *fuck man, I'll just wait until he's all done.*

That's where we were. In the midst of it. No point saying, "Sorry for your loss." Not now. Not yet. Not until it we were all done.

# CHAPTER TWENTY

*0554 hours*

"It was this one, had to be this one." Dave pointed at an apartment.

There were no zombies there, like last time, if it was the right one. Perhaps we'd just killed them all. Very likely. "Why didn't he come out and fight with us?" I said.

Spade stared at the apartment. "We'll go in and check it out. If he's not there, the search is over. We're done. We're going back to the boat and leaving this shit stain harbor. Understood?"

No one argued.

Palmeri stayed behind me, I stood behind Dave, and Spade took point. He waved us on to follow.

Staying low, we crossed between apartments. We reached Marf's and put our backs to the building. Spade held up a fist to tell us we were to wait.

My breath spewed out in visible vapor. My nose was cold, dirty and the tip was numb. I closed my eyes for a moment and sucked in a deep breath. I exhaled and looked to my left.

Crouched, Spade slid along the side of the apartment toward the door. He had his pistol in one hand, hunter's knife in the other. He signaled with his head, so we advanced.

"Open the door on three," he said.

Dave nodded. Hand on the knob.

It was a silent head-bob count. On the third one, Dave pulled open the door.

Spade didn't move. Didn't charge in, nothing.

We waited as seconds ticked by.

I counted them off with the speed of my heartbeat.

Four. Five. Six.

"Marf?" Spade said. It was the softest I'd heard him speak. "Marf?"

Nothing.

"Stay," Spade said. He took a step up and into the apartment.

I looked right, left, right. It felt like we weren't alone. We weren't, just it seemed like things were all around us, closing in and encircling us. I didn't like it.

Spade came back out and tucked the knife into the sheath on his hip. "He got out. No one is in there. Floorboards are torn up. He went out through there."

I sighed. Good for Marfione. He'd made it out.

"So where is he?" Palmeri said. "Why didn't he come to fight with us?"

"Might not have known," Dave said.

That was shit. All the gunshots, Marf would have to be deaf to miss the battle that just finished. "That's not it," I said.

"We aren't looking for him, we can't," Spade said.

I used my radio. "Marfione? Can you hear us, Marf? Over?"

"I said we're not looking. We've been gone far too long as it is. We need to get back to the Coast Guard. Sun will be up soon. Very soon. We can figure out what to do next then," Spade said.

If Marf had answered, I would have disagreed, and gone looking for the soldier, but the radio remained silent.

Spade walked away, back from where we'd just come. "We're going to stay between rows and head straight. Gate can't be more than sixty, seventy yards ahead. We go slowly. We stay packed together. Palmeri, you are the eyes in the back of our head. Understood? Palmeri, do you understand?"

"Roger."

"Okay. We're mobile."

We walked slowly and stayed close. My mind wandered far and fast.


# # #


It had been winter. Calls that were coming into 9-1-1 were few and far between. The fire section had wheeled six of the three-drawer cabinets to the center of the circular pod. Five sat around the makeshift table with poker chips sitting in stacks and piles in front of those playing.

DeJesus shuffled cards.

Milzy, one of first platoon supervisors and the small blind, tossed a chip to the center. "It's hold 'em, right?"

DeJesus nodded. "Correct."

LaForce attempted dancing a chip over knuckles. "They always make this look so easy."

"They practice," Milzy said. "Nothing easy about it. It's why they do it. Frustrates everyone who can't. Rich guys like that probably spend hours in the bathroom mirror doing it over and over and over."

The foghorn-like alarm indicating a new job had been entered activated, came from my terminal. There was a long line on the CAD screen. I read the job text. "HOUSE ON FIRE -- UNKN IF ANYONE INSIDE"

I entered the line of equipment and the set of their firehouse alarm tones. This way, lights and alarms would wake sleeping firemen. Then it would be followed it up with a long alert tone, called Boxing It Out. That way, firemen knew I wasn't just sending them on an EMS run.

My headset was on and my foot depressed the pedal below my desk. I spoke slowly, and clearly. "Telephone alarm report of a house on fire, possible people still inside. Going to be the vacant house across from--" I said, giving the address, the cross streets and named off the three closest engines and two trucks, as well as the rescue and battalion chief to respond.

More information popped up on my monitor.

"It's a backup call, Chase. Fill it out," Milzy said, standing by my shoulder.

I toned out the department, stepped on the pedal, and said, "Backup call for the report of a house fire--possible people trapped." I sent the protectives, fire investigation and deputy chief to the location before the first unit was even on scene.

"Engine Five on scene, two and half story wood frame with flames from the roof. Give me a working fire and restricted alarm," the officer on the engine said over the air.

My job was to parrot reports in case their radio signal was weak. Everyone would hear me fine. "Engine Five on scene of a two and a half wood frame with flames from the roof. Declaring a working fire restricted alarm. Deputy Chief, do you copy?"

"Deputy copies. I'm on scene. I'll take command. Battalion chief has operations."

"Showing the deputy chief on scene. You have command. Battalion chief to have operations." I typed while I spoke.

Job for me now was to stay out of their way. They had a fire to fight. If they needed more equipment, and police for traffic, they'd ask. I'd get it started their way.

"Command to dispatch?"

"Dispatch on, Command."

"We've got heavy flames from the roof, A and B side. Give me a second alarm. Start police and two ALS ambulances. We believe we have three children inside."

My stomach dropped. I balanced up the job as I spoke. "Command reporting heavy flames from the roof, A and B sides. Giving you a second alarm. Starting police and two ALS ambulances. Possibly three children inside," I said.

"I have your ambulances started," LaForce said.

"Second alarm assignment?" Milzy said. He wasn't asking. He wanted to make sure I had it ready to go. I looked at the flow. Command needed another two engines and a truck. I rattled off whom I knew to be next in. Milzy nodded, "Send 'em."

I sent them.

"It's a listed vacant," DeJesus said. "Talked to RG&E. No gas or electricity running."

"Someone had a candle lit," I mumbled. Cold night like tonight? Probably several candles.

Radio squawked with life. It sounded like Darth Vader on the opposite end. It was the air tanks, the mask, their breaths, in and out. "Command, we've got two. Two. Bringing them out now. Both breathing. Repeat both breathing."

"Command to Dispatch."

"Command, go ahead," I said.

"Engine Five is extracting two patients from the vacant. Start a third ambulance as a stand-by."

"Engine Five is extracting two patients from the vacant. Third ambulance for a standby, being started, sir" I said.

All I kept thinking about was the initial report. It had been for three people inside the house. Three. Where was the third? Hiding under a bed? Inside a closet? Unconscious along a wall? In the bathroom?

"Truck Ten to dispatch. Truck Ten has a hole in the floor, second level -- just past the stairs. We are unable to get around it. We cannot complete a search."

I hit an alert tone. "All city companies, Truck Ten reporting a hole in the floor on the second level. Unable to conduct a search. Command copy?"

"Command copies," the deputy chief said. "Command to Truck Ten."

"Truck Ten on for Command."

"Truck Ten, patients are saying the third child was last seen in a crib in an upstairs bedroom to the left of the stairs."

"Truck Ten copies. We're attempting to make our way now to the bedroom."

"Command copies. Command to Rescue?"

"Rescue on, go ahead Command."

"Your location, sir?"

"First floor, inside the structure. We see the hole. It's a big hole, Chief."

"Command copies, Rescue."

The poker game forgotten, Milzy worked on a portable dry erase board. It mapped out where all the engines and trucks were stationed in the city. Proactive. He knew that at any moment the phone would ring. The Deputy Chief would want to move companies around. Can't leave parts of the city bare with so many pieces of equipment tied up on a house fire. He used a grease pencil to scratch off the units on scene and jot down on the right what equipment was left.

Police dispatchers got paid for what they did. They did it over and over every night, and the lot of them had to have carpal tunnel. Fire dispatchers were paid for what they know.

"Truck Ten to Command."

"Command on, go ahead Truck Ten."

There was a pause. We all waited. "Sir, we've got the third victim."

There it was.

Victim.

Not patient.

I felt helpless. I knew the firemen did, too. At least they were there and active. I was sitting on the other side of the radio. My lip quivered some, so I pursed them tightly. I wasn't going to get emotional. I managed to hold it in. There'd be time later, after my shift, on the drive home, but not now.

"You good, McKinney?" Milzy clapped a hand onto my back. He knew. We all knew. A baby had just died in a fire.

"Oh, yeah. All good," I said.

He used his grease pencil on the board. Maybe he was keeping busy so he didn't have to think about what just happened. I pulled up a map on one of the other terminals, plopped the address in and stared at the vacant house. It was daytime in Google. A street view. No fire trucks, no police cars, no ambulances, no fire, no dead baby.

# # #

"The gate." It was Dave.

We were at the back of the last apartment. Dave was right. The gate was dead ahead. "Where are the rest of the zombies?"

"I didn't keep count, but if there were seventy or so, we must have killed most of them, right?" Dave said.

I doubted it, but I said, "Yeah. We must have."

Without ammo, the rifle was merely a bat. I held it in both hands. When I looked back, I saw that Palmeri was doing the same.

"Don't forget your knife," she said.

I looked to my hip. "Never. You ready? We're not out of the woods yet."

She didn't smile. "I'm ready."

# # #

Spade ran, bent forward, staying low. Dave, me and then Palmeri followed. We must have looked like giant ducks.

We reached the fence. I heard it, though.

The growing growl of a zombie moan. It came from behind us.

"Hurry," Spade said.

He stood at the gate and waved us through. Only when I turned around did I see the fast zombies charging.

"Hurry, Palmeri," I said. I don't know if I shouted it. My head was off balance. I thought I might fall. Blood must have rushed to my head. Maybe from being bent over and running, or quite possibly just from being sick and tired of the constant fight during the last week or so.

She passed the gate, running hard, breathing heavily.

Spade rolled the gate closed. A zombie arm made it through. Spade did not hesitate. He slammed it between the fence poles, chopping off the protruding appendage just below the elbow. "Palmeri, hold the gate," he said. "Hold the gate shut!"

She swapped spots with Spade. Did her best to keep the gate closed without having her fingers bitten. "Hurry," she said.

Spade slipped off his belt, laced it through link on the gate, and then along the wall of the fence and buckled it. Tight.

"Unless they can unfasten that, it should hold them," he said.

Don't know why, but I smiled. It was as if we made progress by outsmarting *them*. Kinda felt like outsmarting a dog- -throwing an imaginary ball and they take off after it. I wasn't going to let that spoil the feeling. No. I wanted to relish the small victory. We deserved that much, that little. Showed that as long as the fuckers didn't bite us, we could win. Survive... perhaps.

"Wipe that stupid smile off your face, McKinney. We're not safe yet." Spade spat a wad of shit out of his mouth, wiped his sleeve across his face and took off running along the side of the fence.

Just like that, my little victory was shat on.

The zombies had all made it to the gate. How fucking good for them. They stuck fingers through the links, and noses and tongues.

"Let's go," Palmeri said.

I pulled my knife from the sheath.

"Chase," Dave said.

I jabbed the blade into an eye socket. Black goo oozed. Once I removed the knife, the thing fell to the ground. The others stepped on it. Two creatures looked up, as if they realized they'd just gotten a little closer to the top of the fence.

I killed another by stabbing a blade into its mouth, through the roof, and punching it up to the brain. Then, I used two hands to pull my knife free. This one dropped on top of the other zombie I'd just killed.

The zombies that had looked up before stepped onto this corpse as well. And again, looked up.

"Holy shit," I said.

"Chase, we've got to go. I can't even see Spade anymore."

"Did you see that?" I said.

Palmeri had my arm. "Yeah. You're a real fucking bad ass."

She pulled me along, as we jogged to catch up with Spade.

I think my mouth hung open the whole time with my eyes wide.

There was something else about them, something I couldn't quite remember. Something I should remember. Right now, I was just too mystified by what I'd seen. All I could think, all that just kept running through my mind was, *What the fuck just happened?*

# CHAPTER TWENTY-ONE

*0628 hours*

The sun wouldn't be up for at least another hour. Maybe a little less. It was November, after all. The fire burned, but we were farther from it than before. As we ran along the side of fence perimeter, I saw flames. They didn't rage and fight away the darkness anymore. In fact, they seemed to make everything around it that much blacker. It was as if the fire sucked out the light and left the area in shadows.

We came to the part of the fence where we needed to turn toward the river to go back to the boat. Part of me did not expect to make it back here and that had been a terrible realization I'd faced, buried and attempted to ignore the whole time we'd been at the compound. Felt as if I should drop to my knees and kiss the ground, thankful to be alive, safe and back.

Spade held a finger up to his lips, as if we didn't know by now to keep quiet. He might be an excellent shot, something of a leader, but right now, I was really hating his guts. I did my best not to return an eye roll. I kept my rifle in both hands, my knife back in its home. Staying bent forward, we crossed open area; the worst sound was that of shoes pulling free of the thick mud as we slogged our way through.

Spade stopped and stood up straight, with his arms at his side.

My stomach dropped and the muscles tightened. Something was wrong. He wouldn't be stopped like that. He just wouldn't.

"Boat's fucking gone." He shook his head, raised his arms, and then punched them back down to his sides. "The boat is fucking gone. And so is Spencer. Where the fuck is Spencer."

Spencer had one job, which was to shoot the Captain if he tried to leave with the boat.

I was already doubled over. Vomiting made sense. I held it down, spitting out a mouthful of bile. "Dave?"

Dave was standing by Spade now, looking back at me. "Yeah, it's gone. Mess of bodies on the ground I think. Too dark. I can't tell for sure."

Bodies?

Palmeri and I made it to them and the four of us stood there. We could hear the river, catching glimpses of the current when moonlight hit it right. Dave was correct; the grass around the empty slip was littered with something. Only thing that made sense was bodies.

I started running, but Spade grabbed my arm.

I shrugged it off. "What do you think you're doing?"

"We don't know what's over there," he said. "Look, I know you're upset. This is bad. Okay, bad. But we can't stop being smart because of our emotions. We need to--"

Fuck him. I ran toward the slip.

First lump I encountered was a zombie, as well as the second. I looked back. Palmeri and Dave scoped out the area as well, kicking over dead things for better views.

The corpses stunk. Sifting through a garbage dump in mid-July might have smelled better. Each new one I came across, I stopped before looking at faces, because I didn't want to find...

"Dad? Dad!"

It wasn't a yell, but more of a loud whisper. It came from my left. "Charlene?"

Something ran at me from the darkness.

I knew it was my daughter. I knew it, but I still stood, rifle in hand, ready to swing.

"Daddy!" Charlene said, dropped to her knees.

I let go of the rifle and fell in front of her. She wrapped her arms around me, burying her face into my chest. "Honey, what is it? What's wrong?"

"Cash," she said. "Cash, Daddy."

"Char, tell me what's going on? What happened?" I pulled her head away from me. Dim moonlight allowed me enough glow to see her eyes that were red and puffy. She'd been crying since long before now.

"He's been shot. He got shot. It's my fault."

Her fault?

"Where is he?" I said. "Where's your brother?"

She pointed back the way she'd come. "Over there. Allison has him. She's with him."

It's my fault, ran through my head. I wanted answers. There were too many questions. No time to ask anything. Charlene and I were up, and running. I heard the others behind us, our feet pounding cold, muddy earth.

"Over here," Allison said.

We'd entered a small forest. Charlene led us through pines and leafless maples. To the west, a purple and orange hue spread like a wavy line on the river, across the horizon. Morning was upon us. A new day, and off to a bad fucking start.

I stopped short. Cash lay on the ground with his shirt torn open. Allison sat by his head. Erway kneeled beside him. She used a cloth to apply pressure to the wound. A bullet wound.

It's my fault, Charlene had said. If she shot her brother, it wasn't her fault. It was mine. I let her have a gun. Fourteen and I armed my baby with a gun.

"It's okay." Dave rested a hand on my back. "Don't hold it back, man. Don't hold it in."

I didn't realize I was crying. My knees gave out, but Dave caught me and lowered me to the ground. Cash looked more than vulnerable. He looked peaceful. His skin was wet with sweat, pale, and blue from the cold. "Allison," I said.

"We need to get the bullet out. There's not enough light to do it here," Erway said. "I don't have what we need. A more sterile place would be better."

I didn't even bother looking around. We were in the woods, at the foot of the mountains, surrounded by the river and a camp filled with walking dead zombies. Where the fuck were we going to go that was more sterile. "You can't do it here?" I said.

"I can. Just wouldn't be the best place. As it is, there's going to be a good chance he'll get an infection without antibiotics," she said. I hated her matter-of-fact tone, but was just was telling it like it was and not holding back. I respected it, but just hated her tone.

"Daddy," Charlene said. "We have to save him. It's all my fault! Mine!"

"It's not her fault," Allison said.

"Where the fuck's our boat?" Spade said.

"Not now," Palmeri said.

"What do you mean, not now? We could help the kid on the boat," he said. "Where's our boat?"

"They're gone. Most of them dead. They were going to leave without all of you," Erway said. She looked at me. "Your daughter tried to stop them."

It's why she thought it was her fault. I could see it in Erway's eyes.

"The crewmen managed to get the boat out of the slip, ans headed further up the St. Lawrence," Sues said.

"Okay, okay," I said. I had nothing else. Nothing.

"He been bitten, or is that a gunshot?"

We spun around. Spade was fast, Palmeri, too. They had guns aimed at two strangers, who in turn had rifles aimed at us.

The men wore long beards and flannel under *Carhartt* camouflage coats with matching pants. They were dressed for the elements as well as for hunting. I'd put money on it that these were locals.

"Shot," I said. "He's been shot. Not bitten."

They eyed us for a long moment. "Lower your weapons."

"You first," Spade said.

The men didn't move. "We don't have to. We know your guns are all empty. All of you used every bit of ammo fighting them zombies inside the fenced area back there. Ain't got a single bullet left between the lot of ya."

Seemed no point to arguing. They'd been somewhere safe watching us. Had seen us up against the enemy. Why they hadn't helped…would I have helped? I'd like to think I would have. Good chance I wouldn't have, though. Damned good chance.

"Put them down, guys," I said.

"Not until they do," Spade said.

I hated to do it, take sides. "Guy's right. We don't have ammunition. You're in a standoff with an empty weapon. How do you plan to win that? Put the guns down."

Palmeri did as I asked, first, but Spade held out a few seconds longer. "Spade," I said. I wanted him to understand that I wasn't fucking around. My son was bleeding out over here.

Spade finally lowered his rifle.

As one, the two men lowered theirs. "We've got a camp. Not exactly close, but it's better than trying to dig out a bullet here. Let's get him transported," the one guy said.

"We don't know who either of you are," Spade said.

"That's enough," I said. I wasn't going to yell. Last thing we needed was to get all loud and rowdy, and end up attracting more zombies. We'd be fucked if that happened.

"Not going to be easy to move him," Erway said. "Bullet's in his side. If there isn't internal bleeding, moving him could cause                                                                                  it."
"And doing surgery out here won't make him any better. You're his father, so it's your kid. Your call," the man said.

I looked at Erway. "He has a point."

I nodded. "I'll carry him."

No one argued. I walked on my knees closer to my son. I scooped him up the way I had a million times when he was an infant. Dave helped me up onto my feet. "I've got it now, thanks."

"My brother will lead. You guys follow him. I'll take the rear," the man said. "We've got to move fast. There are herds scattered all around. Lot of them fast-running kinds, too. You know the ones I mean?"

We all did. "Lead the way," I said.

Cash's head, arms and legs dangled limp; dead weight in my arms. I'd spent the better part of yesterday with him on my back, arms around my neck. At nine, he wasn't that light but light enough, I guess, and I was thankful. Carrying him this way, though, tugged at my emotions. I bit my lip hard to keep it all in check. I needed strength and the only way I'd get it was by not paying attention to what I was actually doing.

"He breathing?" Allison said.

"I don't know," I said, running faster.

"I don't think he's breathing," she said.

"Erway," I said. I stopped, set him down and put my ear to his lips. "I can't tell. I don't know."

Erway dropped down beside me and pushed me out of the way. She lowered her head to his face. She seemed to watch for his chest to rise and fall while listening for breathing. "He's breathing. Shallow breaths, but breathing."

The man from the rear came up on us. "Why'd we stop?"

"How far is this camp?" Erway said. "Because I'm not sure we can wait."

"Right up that hill," the man said. He handed his rifle over to me, squatted down and lifted my son into his arms. "We'll get him there. Come on!"

We all followed. I was now the one with the gun with ammo. I was last. Ahead of me was Charlene and Allison, they stayed right by the man with my son. Erway was behind them. Dave, Sues and Crystal were ahead of everyone, must have been right behind the other guy on point.

Didn't want to jinx anything, but we'd not seen a zombie in a while. That was another thing that I suddenly found myself feeling thankful about.

# CHAPTER TWENTY-TWO

*0718 hours*

The log cabin sat on top of the hill we'd just climbed. The horizontally laid logs interlocked at the corners, while the logs making up the purlin roof were notched into the gable-wall logs. Tall pines and a variety of trees were set back, but surrounded the patch of property.

"Get him inside," the one brother said to the man carrying my son.

Everyone shuffled in.

"Pull the blanket off my bed, Jeremy. And someone, shut and lock that door," the man said. He followed his brother to a room. Jeremy stripped the bedding as the other man laid my son down onto the mattress.

Erway set her bag down beside the bed. "Do you have a bowl I can use to sterilize my equipment? A jug of water and some clean towels, or sheets."

"I'll grab it, Jason. You stay here," Jeremy said. "You stay."

Jason gave me a pat on the back as he squeezed by me and out of the room. Allison, Charlene and I moved closer to the bed.

"I don't need all three of you in here," Erway said. "Chase, you stay. I am going to need your help."

"I'm not going anywhere," Charlene said. She had her arms around Allison's waist. They both actually held each other.

"Take her out of here, Alley," I said.

"I'm staying, Dad! I'm not—"

"Get her out of here!"

Allison didn't have to try too hard to remove my daughter from the room. Charlene was spent, emotionally, and physically.

Jeremy returned with a couple of porcelain bowls. "I brought rubbing alcohol, too."

Jason took the supplies. "What should I do?"

Erway used scissors to cut away Cash's clothing. "Pour the alcohol into the bowls. Set them on the nightstand by me. Chase, get on the other side of the bed. I'm going to need you to hold his arm and legs down. He's passed out right now, but without any anesthetics, if he wakes up, any movement is going to be dangerous. We understand each other?"

I nodded. She took one of the towels and pressed it over the small hole in my son's stomach, and mopped up far too much blood.

"You two, I'm going to need you to hold down his arm and leg on this side, without getting in my way. You, take the arm. And you, you have his leg," she said.

Like me, they nodded.

"You've done this before," I said. "Removed a bullet?"

She smiled. "I'm a paramedic."

That was hardly an answer. Maybe I didn't want an answer as bad as I thought I needed one.

Erway placed silver tools into the bowls of alcohol. "I need to wash my hands," she said.

"That way, right around the corner," Jason said.

"You hold this cloth tight on the wound," Erway said, placing my hand onto the towel. "Don't lift it to look at it. Got it? Hold it. Firmly."

"Seems like the doc has it together," Jason said. "That's a good thing."

Small talk wasn't going to cut it. My mind ached. I looked over my son' body. The towel seemed to do little more than keep blood from staining Jason's bed.

Erway returned, removed plastic gloves from her bag and snapped them on over her hands. "I could use more light."

It was the first time I noticed wood shutters on the inside of the cabin locked in place over the two windows in the room. "Can we open one of them?" Jeremy said. "Sun's up. Be the best light."

Jason nodded. They each went to a window. "My brother built this place so sunlight would hit the cabin whenever there was sunlight to be had."

I ignored him, as we all did. "Now what?" I said.

"Get ready to hold him. Chase, remove the towel," she said, so I did.

She poured some water from the jug over the wound. The hole didn't look so bad with all the blood gone. I almost smiled.

From the bowl of alcohol, she removed what looked like scissors. "What's that?" Jason said.

"Hemostat," she said. "Now shh!"

Outside the room, I heard Allison and Charlene sobbing.

"Good chance he's going to stir, wake up," she said.

"It's going to hurt?" I said.

"Immensely." She chose something that was long and slender. It looked like a pick a dentist used to scrape at plaque build-up, but was thicker all around. She stuck it into the gaping hole.

Cash didn't just stir. He woke the fuck up. His eyes went wide, darting left and right and then stopped on me. His mouth was in a giant "O." He looked like he wanted to scream, but the sound was trapped inside his lungs.

"I'm searching for the bullet. I'm flicking the probe," she said. "I'll hear a click when I've found it."

Cash found his voice. He screamed. His body shook.

I held his arm down with both hands, but just barely. Jason had both of his legs and he was practically laying out over them, his chest weighing them down. Jeremy had the other arm, and sat with his back to the bed, holding on as best he could.

"Hang in there, buddy. We're almost done," I said. "You're doing great. Great. She's almost done."

"Think I found it," Erway said.

Blood spilled from the round hole. I didn't want to think about the possibility of internal injuries from the bullet.

Erway moved the probe around, as if she was trying to hook the bullet and hoist it out. When she stopped, she used the other hand with the hemostat, and opened the tongs slightly. She dipped them into the wound with the probe and Cash thrashed.

"You have to hold him still," she said.

"We're trying," Jason said.

"Try harder," she said.

"Cash? Cash, buddy, we're almost done. It's almost over," I said. There was little more I could say. He wasn't talking or responding. He was just screaming.

Then he stopped screaming. His body stopped writhing. "Erway," I said.

"He passed out."

"He what?" I said.

"The pain. He passed out," she said. That tone again. "I want to get the bullet now, while he's out. Should be a little easier."

Easier. I almost laughed.

Then she flicked a little more with the probe, as if guiding the bullet up toward the tongs of the hemostat. She clipped and cursed, then clipped again. "Shit," she said. "Jeremy, pour some more water over the entry point, there."

Jeremy looked reluctant to let go of Cash's arm. He tentatively let go with one hand and stared for a moment – like he was afraid that my son's arm would snap out and latch onto his throat.

"Jeremy, water!"

He picked up the jug and poured out water. "That enough?"

"More," she said.

The blood thinned when mixed with water and rolled off his skin. "Okay, that's good."

I didn't think I'd be able to watch anymore. With Cash out of it, it was a little easier.

Erway's mouth opened. She looked at me. "Got it."

With a steady hand, she slowly withdrew the hemostat, which had a flattened slug in its grip. "That all of it?" I said.

"Not sure yet." She dropped it into a glass on the nightstand. "Looks like a .22. I was able to pull it straight out. That's good."

The bedroom door opened and Dave popped his head in. "Chase, we got zombies in the yard. A lot of zombies."

# CHAPTER TWENTY-THREE

Erway assured me she could finish up on Cash without us.

"I've got guns," Jason said. "Come with me."

I stopped at the doorway, "You're good?"

"We're going to be fine," Erway said. She even smiled. That made me the most apprehensive. All along, it had been the tone that bothered me. The tone, that was honest. I knew where she stood. She wasn't feeding me bullshit. The smile, that fucked with me. A mental fuck at that.

The whole downstairs of the cabin had shutters over the windows. The shutters were on the inside. I liked it. Zombies, if they could, had to first break the glass, and then figure out a way through the wood shutters. Door was solid and locked. Place was like a fortress. "Guns?" I said.

"Here," Jason said.

Hall closet. Jeremy pulled open the door.

"How is he, Dad?" Charlene asked.

"Erway got the bullet. I think he's going to be okay," I said.

Charlene's lower lip quivered. "I'm so sorry," she said. "I got mad at the captain and I shot him. I shot him and then his crew started shooting at us. But they were going to leave. He was going to leave you and everyone else stranded out there."

"It's okay, honey. I'm not mad," I said. It wasn't going to be enough. I needed to give her more. She needed more. "I'm proud of you. You stood up for me. You did the right thing."

Vitale had tried to station Spencer by the boat to prevent just such a thing from happening. Where had he been? What had gone wrong there?

She hugged me.

I looked at the closet, but clearly, it was no closet. Dave disappeared inside, with Sues behind him, Palmeri and Crystal. It must lead to another room. The cabin didn't look that big when we came up on it. I'll admit I'd been preoccupied with Cash. With everything. Feeling overwhelmed was becoming the norm, and I didn't like it.

"Come on," I said. I took Charlene's hand and led her to the doorway. I went in first and emerged into a room that looked like something out of a movie. AK-47s lined one wall. Gun safe doors stood open showcasing a variety of rifles and shotguns. Another wall held both compound and recurve bows over a work table where it looked like feather fletching were homemade and affixed to arrow shafts. The floor was stockpiled with pallets and boxes of ammunition, and there was no shortage of swords, hatchets and machetes.

After using guns the last day and a half, many might disagree, but I prefer the machetes and swords. You didn't run out of steel the way you did ammo. You could only carry so many rounds with you. I'd take a gun or two, stuff my pockets with ammo, but I wanted to get my hands on the machetes and swords, and strap them around my waist, and to my back. That's what I was thinking.

"Seen this coming?" Palmeri said. She slowly spun in circles, as if trying to take it all in. I had to agree that it was a lot to process.

"Yes," Jeremy said. "Not zombies, but something. Fall of the government. Got democrats and bleeding heart liberals running things. It was bound to happen sooner or later. Not zombies."

"You said that, not zombies," Jason said. "We believe there is nothing wrong with stockpiling a little peace of mind. This room, everything inside here, it's our peace of mind."

Jeremy bounced up and down. "Got another room, twice the size of this room with all kinds of food, and water, and sup—"

"Enough, Jeremy," Jason said.

Jason was the big brother. That much was evident. And the smart one. He didn't like his little brother giving away too much. After all, we were strangers.

"Take what you think you'll need. Got bars on the outside of the windows upstairs. No shutters. Be a perfect place to hit targets out on the lawn," Jason said.

I couldn't agree more. We grabbed what we thought we would need. I fit a belt around my waist, and affixed both a broadsword on one side, and a twelve inch blade recurve hunting knife on the other. I slung a machete in a leather sheath over my neck and shoulder. The blade had to have been twenty-five inches long.

Charlene stood beside me and I looked at her. "What are you doing?" I said.

"You don't want me to have a gun," she said.

"You're right. I don't. Wish things could be like they were before. When there were no...no zombies. That's not where we are anymore, honey. We're far, far away from that place, from that time. I don't want you to have a gun, but what happened to your brother—that wasn't your fault. You've shown me over and over that you are responsible, and that you can handle the truth and handle what is going on. I don't want you to have a gun, but Char, I *need* you to have one," I said.

"Chase! Chase!"

It was Erway. Charlene and I locked eyes.

We left the weapons room and ran back for the bedroom. Erway was at the door. "He's awake."

I studied her expression. She gave nothing away.

Charlene grabbed my hand. It wasn't subtle. She was telling me there was no way she wasn't coming into the room this time.

We walked in. I pointed to the right side of the bed. Charlene went there. "Hey, little brother," she said.

She couldn't hold it together. The tears rolled down her cheeks, but she smiled. She wore a mask made of smiles.

I took the left side of the bed and knelt there. Took his hand. "Hey, buddy," I said.

"Dad," he said.

"Yeah, Cash, what?"

"Did you kill my mother?"

It wasn't the question that I expected. I stared at him, felt Charlene staring at me.

"You came looking for us, right?"

"Of course, I did," I said.

"Where did you go, when you were looking for us?" His words came out slow. A whisper. His lips were dry, cracked. "Where did you look for us? You went to Mom's house, didn't you?"

"Yes, Cash, I did."

"When you got there, did you kill my mom?"

I looked up and over at Charlene. She seemed to wait for the answer, too. They did not need to hear the truth.

"No," I said. "I did not. I didn't kill her."

Charlene's eyes narrowed. She didn't believe me. I saw it in my head. Their mom on the bed, the shattered picture frame on the hardwood floor. I used a shovel. Tried to flatten her skull with it, but swing after swing had done little to stop her until I used the blade of the shovel and separated most of her head from her shoulders.

I cringed. The memory felt horrible, and knew I'd relive it time and again once this nightmare ended. If it ever ended.

I had to give more. "When I got there, we searched the house for you guys. For the two of you. We found your mom's husband," I said.

"I had to chop his hand off," Charlene said. Was she smiling?

"We killed him. We had too. But when I was upstairs, I found your mother," I said. "She was in one of the bedrooms, looking at a picture of you kids…"

She had been in a bedroom looking at a picture.

The zombies at the fence had figured out how to climb higher by standing on corpses like step stools.

"Dad," Charlene said.

I hadn't killed their mother. What I did might have been worse. Don't think I ever expected them to ask me about it. Not sure, I'd have handled it differently, regardless. "I left her there," I said. "I closed the bedroom door. I left her in the room with pictures of you two."

"Do you think that made her happy," Cash said.

I closed my eyes. "Yes, buddy. I think that made her happy. She has memories of you guys to keep her happy."

Memories. In her infected state, did she have memories? Was it possible?

"Is he sleeping?" Charlene said. "Dad?"

I watched his chest. It didn't rise. It didn't fall. "Erway," I said. "He's not breathing!"

# CHAPTER TWENTY-FOUR

I'd been sound asleep when Julie woke me up with a nudge. Working two jobs, when I had time to sleep, I slept.

"What is it?" I'd whispered. Don't think I'd even opened my eyes.

"The baby," my ex-wife had said. Charlene was five years old. Hardly a baby.

"What does she want?"

"Not Charlene. This baby," she said.

I opened my eyes. Julie had the bedroom light on. She was dressed, her packed bag for the hospital by the door. "Is it time?"

She shrugged. "Contractions started about an hour ago. They're less than three minutes apart already."

"Why didn't you wake me?" I said, lifting myself up onto an elbow.

"If it was nothing, I would have let you sleep. I assumed they wouldn't get so close together so soon." She stood by her bag, with one hand on the doorknob.

"Doctor told us the second delivery will be faster than the first. Your body already knows the routine. Dilating and effacing," I said, and threw off the bedspread. "I have time to shower?"

"I don't think so. I waited as long as I could."

I picked up the phone, "I'll call our parents and get Charlene ready. You sit down, just rest. Try to relax."

A contraction must have hit, because her face contorted. She gave the doorknob a white-knuckle grip. She breathed quick, shallow breaths in a steady rhythm.

I jumped up and led her back to the bed. "Sit, please. Just sit."

I called my mother first. She said she'd call Julie's parents. Everyone would meet at the hospital.

"Okay. Keep doing your breathing. I'm going to dress Charlene," I said. I went from our room to Charlene's. We'd need a bigger place. This two-bedroom ranch was not going to cut it. Having Charlene sleep in her own room only just happened. With a crib in there now, she'd never get any rest while sharing space with a baby.

I stood over her bed. She was balled up under blankets. Strands of hair were sticky with sweat and stuck to her face. A hug-pillow was between her arms. The hug-pillow that I'd bought for her. I had one, too. So when she slept in her own bed like a big girl, she could hug her pillow, and I would hug mine, and it would be like we were napping together. It didn't just make her happy; it made me happy.

I wondered how happy she'd be to have a little brother or sister?

I peeled back the blanket, but she didn't stir. "Charlene," I said. "Honey?"

Her eyelids fluttered before opening. "Daddy?"

"We need to get up, get ready. Mommy is going to have the baby today."

Her eyes opened wider and she sat up. "The baby's coming now?"

I nodded.

She got right out of bed. I watched, amazed, as she changed her clothes and grabbed her suitcase on wheels. "I'm ready!"

"What's in the suitcase?" I said.

"I have toys, puzzles, books, sippy-boxes and snacks. Mommy said it could take a long time, so I should pack things to keep me busy."

I kissed her nose. "Mommy is a genius!"

The hospital was less than seven miles away. It took us nearly twenty minutes to get there. It was just after midnight, so there was no traffic. We did catch every red light, but mainly because I drove thirty miles an hour, and as soon as I saw amber light, I slowed to a stop. Was I a little apprehensive about getting into an accident? Yeah, you could say I was.

We pulled into Emergency. At the sliding doors, I stopped the car. I helped both women out and grabbed a lone wheelchair. "Sit. I'm going to park right over there," I said. "Char, take care of your mom until I get back."

I parked, hurried over the sliding doors and pushed Julie into the hospital, her bag on my shoulder, while Charlene followed alongside, wheeling her suitcase.

"Chase," Julie said in a whisper. I lowered my head as I wheeled us to the front desk, past security. "I haven't felt the baby since we left the house."

"He's resting between contractions," I said.

"Chase, something's wrong."

I stopped at the desk. The woman there stared at the three of us. My wife had her hand on her bulbous belly.

"We need to see a doctor. Our doctor. Julie, did you tell our doctor we were coming to the hospital?"

"I did. I called him just before I woke you up," she said.

"We need to see our doctor, please. He's going to deliver our baby," I said.

The woman smiled. "What is your doctor's name?"

Brain fart. I had no clue.

"Give me my bag," Julie said. I did. She unzipped it and took out some forms. "Everything is there. Admittance forms are all filled out."

"Mom's a genius," Charlene said.

My parents entered the hospital and I walked Charlene over. "We're going to be going in. She's got stuff inside the suitcase to keep her busy."

"And I brought a pocket full of change for the vending machines," my father said. He took Charlene by the hand. "We'll be fine."

My mother gave me a kiss. "How's Julie?"

"Says the baby isn't moving," I said.

My mother shook her head. "Everything's fine. Go be with her."

I joined Julie as she was being wheeled through automated doors that had swung open.

Once in a delivery room, the nurse hooked Julie up to a baby heart monitor. We all watched the blips dance across the screen as a roll of receipt-like paper steadily spit out of an opening. The nurse tore off about ten inches of paper.

"How's it look?" I said.

"The doctor will be right in to explain things. In the meantime, please change into the hospital gown," the nurse said, smiled, and left the room with the printout.

"Hate when they do that," Julie said, pulling off her clothing. "She knows what the monitor says."

I just nodded, helping her into the flower print gown. No point arguing over what a nurse can and can't tell patients.

We didn't wait long before a doctor entered the room, but it wasn't Julie's obstetrician. She looked at the monitor as she said hello and introduced herself.

"Julie, if I can have you place your legs in the stirrups, please."

I stepped aside.

The doctor parted Julie's knees.

I focused on Julie, keeping my eyes on hers. They were open too wide. The fear oozed from her expression.

"Last time you felt the baby move, or kick?"

"Just before we left the house. Almost an hour," Julie said.

"Everything okay?" I said.

The doctor ignored me. "We're going to perform a cesarean delivery. Nothing to be worried about. The baby's heart is beating a little fast. Suggests he's under some stress is all. Possibly while he was moving around, getting ready to be delivered, he managed to get a little tangled up with the umbilical cord."

A man with a bed on wheels entered the room with another man behind him.

"But what about my doctor? He's not here," Julie said.

"I just spoke to him. He will be here in a few minutes and will join me in surgery. Mr. McKinney, we will show you where to scrub up and change into surgical greens," the doctor said.

My stomach dropped. I pretended it had not and clapped my hands together. "Okay. Let's do this," I said.

I wasn't fooling anyone. Julie just stared at me. Her hand was on my arm. "Chase."

"Everything is going to be fine."

The orderlies, or transport techs--whatever , moved Julie from the bed she was in to the one with wheels, pushed her out of the room and I followed.

In the operating room, both doctors stayed on one side of a drape that separated Julie at the shoulders. We could hear the operation taking place, but could not watch what was being done.

I spoke softly to my wife the whole time. Told her repeatedly that everything was going to be fine, and that I loved her. She cried the entire time. Her eyes were closed and tears just spilling down her cheeks.

When a baby cried, my breath caught in my lungs.

Julie opened her eyes. Her lips moved, but no words came out.

I felt heat in my face. My eyes watered.

Our doctor came around the drape with our baby in his arms. He lowered his cloth mask. "It's a boy!"

"A b-boy," I said. Now, there was no way to hold back the crying.

"He's okay?"

"He was definitely fighting with the umbilical cord. We're going to give him some extra air, but he should be just fine," he said.

"Can I see him?" Julie said.

The doctor handed the baby to me.

His little eyes were open. "He's awake," I said, and leaned as closely to Julie as I could.

"You scared us," Julie said. "You scared me so bad."

# # #

"Chase, your daughter needs you," Erway said.

I was hugging my son. Holding him in my arms. Pressing him tightly to my chest. In my head, over and over, I kept thinking that everything is going to be fine. Everything is going to be fine.

Charlene was still on the other side of the bed, her face buried in the sheets, her sobs muffled by the mattress.

"Chase," Erway said. "Go to your daughter."

"I can't," I said, "I can't put him down. Don't make me put him down."

She put hands on my shoulders. "Chase, your son is gone. Charlene needs you."

He had been so tiny when he was born. "We need to fix this. You need to help him," I said.

Erway left me. She knelt next to Charlene. "Come here, baby," she said.

Charlene lifted her head. Her eyes were swollen, red.

I rocked back and forth with Cash in my arms.

"Daddy," she said.

I couldn't put him down.

"Daddy, please."

When I couldn't move, Erway hugged my daughter.

## Chapter Twenty-Five
*2120 hours*

"Hey, honey."

I opened my eyes. A dream. It had all been a dream. "Alley," I said.

The dark room had a trace of light from the hall; it spilled in through a triangle slice between the open door and the wall.

I didn't recognize the room.

Where was I?

Cash?

"Cash?" I said.

When I heard my voice, I knew. It was no dream. Cash was dead.

Allison hugged me.

"Where's Charlene?" I said.

"Downstairs. Everyone is. The Terrigino brothers made us stew. Squirrel stew." She laughed.

"I don't think I can go down there right now."

"You have to eat, Chase."

It seemed like it had been days since my last meal. Might have been. The idea of eating didn't appeal to me. Not right now. I knew what I needed to do. "I have to bury my son."

"It's dark out. It's late. There could be zombies out there," she said, and took my hand. "Chase, Charlene is hurting badly. You should go downstairs and eat. Sit with her."

Allison was right. Of course she was. How did I ignore my daughter's pain earlier? "Where is she?"

"She's been sitting by a window. I sat next to her for a while, figured she'd fall asleep, but she didn't. She just stared at nothing, really. Just kept on staring. It frightened me. I'm worried about her. You know she thinks this is all her fault. She needs you to tell her that it's not."

"I did. I told her that."

"Chase," Alley said.

"Help me out of here," I said. I didn't have the strength to sit up on my own.

Allison led me to the stairs. "The Terrigino's have been very nice. Generous. Elysia and Crystal have been helping with the stew."

"You said it was…"

"Squirrel."

I cringed.

"Smells good."

"Is that what I smell now?" I said. "Then you have horrible schnozzle on your face. That smells exactly like squirrel."

Allison laughed.

I tried to smile. I knew what needed to be done. Faking it. I needed to fake things from now on. Half of my entire purpose was gone. Dead. It would be near impossible to ever again function as whole.

As we got to the bottom of the stairs, I saw two things right away. The bedroom door where my son died was closed. Across from it, sitting on the ledge of a bay window, Charlene hugged her knees to her chest.

"Hey, baby," I said.

Her head spun around. For just a moment, she looked at me. I worried I'd lost her. My neglect had frozen her heart toward me. I took a step toward her, my arms out in an attempt to apologize, when she climbed off the sill and ran at me. She wrapped arms tight around my neck.

"Daddy, I'm so sorry. I--I'm so sorry," she said.

Allison gave my back a rub and made her way around us.

I sat my daughter down on the stairs, and then I sat next to her. I took her hands in mine. "Baby, it wasn't your fault. I told you that."

"I started all the shooting. I shot that Captain."

"I know. You told me. You had a reason," I said.

"Not a good enough one. He could have left. Taken his boat and left. All we had to do was get off. I didn't have to shoot him. Because I couldn't control my temper, Cash is gone. He's dead because of me," she said.

I had to let go of her hands to wipe tears from her face, and brush hair from her eyes. "Charlene, you did nothing wrong. We're going to get through this. Together, okay. In time, everything will be fine."

It will never, ever be the same, I thought. And I really didn't think everything would be fine, either. It was part of who I was now. A faker. An actor. I even smiled at my daughter as I lifted her chin. "I love you," I said, which was true. "And we are going to get through this. All of this."

"How?" she said.

How.

No idea. None at all.

"What do we do next?" she said.

"I think for starters, we stay here for a bit, get some rest and some food. I think I saw an actual bathroom up there, so we can take a shower," I said.

"One down here, too. Not too shabby for a log cabin," she said.

"It's a downright castle as far as I'm concerned," I said, gave her a half smile. If I turned it up anymore, she'd know it wasn't genuine. She'd call me out, point and accuse me of over-acting. "You eat yet?"

She put a hand on her stomach. "I couldn't."

"Me either. But I think that's what we should do now." I was about to stand up, but she stopped me.

"Dad."

"Yeah, honey?"

"About Allison -- I never really gave her much of a chance," she said.

"I never really brought her around you guys much. When it was my weekends, my days with you guys, I didn't want to have to divide my attention."

"I know. I knew that's what you were doing. The times she did do stuff with us, I was not nice. I mean, I was never mean to her. She'd catch me looking her up and down, or maybe finishing a little sneer," she said. "I didn't like her. Not for you."

"I'm sorry you felt that way," I said. "I was just always alo-_"

"No, Dad. What I'm saying is, that wasn't fair. Of me. I knew you were alone. Working, and doing nothing. And then happy when you had Cash and I. I knew that. I was just jealous. Once you met Allison, I knew that you weren't thinking about us all the time anymore. I felt like," the tears started again, "I felt like we weren't as important to you anymore."

Why it was different with their mother, I had no idea. She was the one who wanted out of the marriage. The one who wanted to be with Douglas, or Donald, or whatever his name was. Why didn't Charlene feel that way about him? Her?

Maybe she did, or had.

"Charlene," I said.

"Just let me finish. Since we've all been together, Allison has been nothing but great. She's done a ton of hand holding and comforting. She sat with me for hours by the window while you slept, which was nice and everything, but what I liked about it most? She didn't say anything. She didn't talk at all. She didn't try to reach out, other than by just being there with me." She kissed me on the cheek. "I like her, Dad. I'm glad she's part of our family."

Charlene stood up, wiped her hands down her jeans, and then held them out to me. I took them, and she pulled me up onto my feet. "You know they made us squirrel stew?"

"You don't say," I said. "Smells…mmmm…unique."

Charlene laughed.

A real laugh. She hugged me again and I held her tight. I never wanted to release her. I needed to find a way to protect her for the rest of her life. There had to be a way. I'd find it, if it was the last thing I did. I'd find a way to keep her safe forever.

# CHAPTER TWENTY-SIX

The stew was not terrible. Gamey and you knew you were eating a large rodent. The freshly diced vegetables and thick broth helped considerably. The dining room table inside the log cabin was long, and like the house, handmade.

I sat on one side between my daughter and Allison. Next to Allison was Crystal. Across from us were Dave, Sues, Palmeri and Spade. At the heads were the Terrigino brothers, Jeremy and Jason. Erway, a vegetarian, ate some carrots and potatoes while helping prepare the meal, and was now sound asleep on a sofa in the other room.

Allison didn't seem to mind it, either. Charlene ate everything in front of her.

Dave and Sues stayed quiet during dinner. They sat close, but neither said a single word. I couldn't figure them out. They'd bonded in such a weird way. It worked for them, but it kind of creeped me out.

"That was delicious," Dave said. He set his napkin on his bowl and pushed back a little in his chair. I couldn't tell if he meant it or not. Perhaps acting ran in our "family."

Jason stood, "Would you like more? We have plenty."

"I honestly don't think I could eat another bite," he said.

I wanted to applaud. Another actor indeed. Bravo. He'd told the truth, but in such a witty way as to not offend our gracious hosts.

"How about you, dear?" Jason looked at Sues.

She dabbed her napkin at the corners of her mouth. "Are you sure there is enough? I would not want to appear rude by taking the last of your stew."

Jason smiled. "My pleasure."

He took her bowl and disappeared into the kitchen with it.

Dave and I looked at each other. He arched an eyebrow. I almost laughed out loud.

Jason returned, steam rising from a rounded full bowl of squirrel stew.

"Oh, that's too much," she said.

"Eat what you can."

"I'll never finish all of this. It would be a sin to waste food, especially during times like they are now," she said.

"Whatever you don't eat, I'll finish," Dave said.

Again, I had to hold back a laugh. Because he still arched that eyebrow at me.

"Well, there you go. Enjoy," Jason said.

We all watched Sues shake out her napkin and place it back on her lap.

"How about anyone else?" Jason said.

We all, at once, politely declined.

"How long have you and your brother been living up here?" Allison said.

Jason took a sip of water. "Our grandfather owned a parcel of land out here. Spent his life clearing it. When he died, our father began building the log house. His dream was to move his family from Nova Scotia down to the states and live off the land."

"Problem was," Jeremy said, "he wasn't a rich man. Had to work. Only had so much time to dedicate to building the place. Jason and I helped as much as we could. Loved coming down here with him. He taught us not just how to build, but how to live off the land. We'd spend long weekends and holidays working here."

"Drove our mother crazy," Jason said.

"His heart gave out. Jason and I were with him. We didn't have any way to get help, or call for an ambulance. We didn't have cell phones then. Papa wouldn't have allowed them even if they were around."

"Place didn't even have electricity at that point," Jeremy said.

They weren't far from a state park. There had to be park rangers, a main office, or a phone somewhere close. I wondered how old they were when the heart attack struck? Had to have been horrible for them.

"He was out in the woods. Been gone, I don't know, an hour or so?" Jeremy said.

Jason nodded. "Sounds about right. Nothing unusual about it. I mean, we were in the wild, really. Nature. Someone's gone for a spell; you don't get all panicked. This wasn't the city. I don't know though, I guess we started to figure something might not be right and went looking for him."

Jeremy stood up, picked up his bowl, and silverware. "Just wasn't right."

"Was nothing we could do. His skin was blue and cold. He'd been dead a while," Jason said.

The room fell silent. Jeremy brought his dirty dish into the kitchen, and to be alone, I presumed.

"The land became ours And our mother's. She wanted nothing to do with it, because she felt like the land was cursed. Our grandfather died on his way here, I guess. We didn't know him. Just what our father told us." Jason looked around, as if admiring the rafters and quality of the completed work. "Two generations of Terrigino men died here. Tried to tell our mother, wasn't going to happen to Jeremy and me. We were younger, and stronger. When we finished building the place, we begged her to come see it, but she wouldn't. Wouldn't even look at pictures of the place. When I say she washed her hands of this land, I mean she scrubbed away even the *idea* of soil from under her nails."

"The place is absolutely breathtaking," Allison said.

"Thank you, dear. I appreciate that. My family appreciates that," Jason said.

Jeremy emerged from the kitchen. "We don't really have anything for dessert. I'm sorry about that. I'd have made Jell-O, or something."

"Please, that's all right," Palmeri said.

I watched Spade. He'd been as quiet as Dave and Sues during dinner. He'd eaten silently, and just seemed to be taking everything in. It wasn't that I didn't trust him, or know him, for that matter, but I felt like he was up to something. I just wished I knew what.

"But, I can brew us up some coffee. Would anyone care for a cup?"

Coffee did sound amazing. As much as I would love a cup, I didn't want anything to hinder my sleep. There was no denying that it felt safe in here. The log cabin was like a fortress with enough weapons, and apparently food, to make anyone lower their guard and relax a little.

Only thing that would be better than a cup of coffee is a pack of cigarettes. Still missed the one Marfione had given me, the one I'd tucked behind my ear to smoke later, but never got the chance. I'd give most anything to have that cigarette back.

"I would love some," Charlene said. She quickly added, "If it's no trouble."

"If it were trouble, dear, I'd not have offered."

Spade's jaw tensed. A ripple made its way up his cheek as if he'd ground his teeth together. I missed it. Something caused the reaction. I looked around casually; certain something was taking place that I just wasn't seeing.

Jeremy stood half inside the dining room, half in the kitchen, his back and shoulder kept the swinging door from swinging. "I will just--"

Erway ran into the room. "Zombies are scratching at the windows!"

# CHAPTER TWENTY-SEVEN

My weapons were upstairs in the bedroom, the machete, sword and the knife.

Everyone else seemed to have a rifle leaning against the wall behind their chair.

"My rifle's in the other room," Charlene said. "Near the window."

She wasn't going anywhere without me right next to her.

Allison checked her clip and slapped it in place. "Let's go get it," she said.

Jason patted the air with both hands. "Everyone, everyone, please. Please, just settle down. It happens sometimes. The smell attracts them when we cook."

"Because you are such a wonderful chef," Jeremy said.

Jason bobbed his head side-to-side, mulling over the compliment. "I suppose so. I suppose. Thing is, ain't none of them things getting in here. I explained the windows, the bars, and the shutters. The doors are steel, and so are the door casings. They'd have to have dynamite to blast them in. Huffing and puffing won't do shit. That, I promise you."

"So, what do we do?" Spade said.

Jason looked at Jeremy. "Will the coffee be long?"

"I'll make it now," he said, and went into the kitchen.

"Coffee," Palmeri said. "You still want coffee?"

"Dear," Jason said, addressing Erway, "the zombies--you look out the window?"

"I saw them, yes."

"How many? Guess."

"Ten, twelve. It was dark," she said.

"If you'd like, if it will make you all feel better, follow me upstairs. Okay?" Jason got up from the table. He wiped his mouth on his napkin, dropped it over his bowl and left the room.

We sat, staring at each other, not exactly sure what to do next.

"Well, are you coming?" Jason said. I could see him from where I sat at the table. He had one foot on the stairs, a hand on the railing, and was leaning back to look at us in the dining room.

Spade motioned us to move along with his rifle. Dave and Sues went first, Crystal behind them.

"You two stay right next to me," I said to Allison and Charlene. I made eye contact with Spade. "Something going on?"

Spade pointed with two fingers at the kitchen, and then shushed me.

Dammit. Something was wrong. He either knew, or sensed something that I was totally missing. I felt the hairs on the back of my neck stand. That was not good. Not at all.

I led Allison and Charlene out of the kitchen, and Palmeri and Spade followed.

Charlene snatched up her rifle by the window. "Why are we going upstairs?"

"You'll see," Jason said. He was already upstairs. Charlene had practically whispered. How had he heard her?

We climbed the stairs. I was behind Palmeri, but ahead of Alley and Charlene. Spade followed along. He kept looking back. I knew this, because I kept looking back at him. It was as if he expected Jeremy to come at him with a kitchen hatchet or something.

I ducked into the room I'd slept in. My belt was on the chair by the bed. I strapped it on. The sword and knife already felt like a part of my body. I slipped my head under the shoulder harness, and sighed with the machete affixed to my back.

"All set?" Allison said.

"Don't think I'm ever taking these off again."

"Think we get to keep them?" Charlene said.

Was a good question.

In a bedroom toward the front of the cabin, Jason had raised one of the windows. "The bars will keep the zombies out even if they managed to climb up the side of the cabin like Spiderman."

Leaning against the wall was rifle with a scope and a silencer screwed on to the barrel.

"When Jeremy and I were younger, we'd come up here with .22s and shoot at beavers, woodchucks, and squirrels. Whatever was out there, you know. We'd just pull a chair up to the window and…" He aimed his rifle out through the slatted bars, and pretended to shoot. "…ping, ping, ping. Just pick off rodents. Were some great times. Truly amazing memories. Thing is that whatever we shot, we ate. Father taught us that. So after we'd hunted, we'd go down and collect up the carcasses, gut 'em, skin em, and bleed 'em. Stews and jerky were two of the things we made regularly."

That awkward silence fell over the room once again as we watched Jason, who now seemed lost in reflection. I wanted to grab him by the shoulders and give him a shake or maybe yell in his face, *What the fuck is wrong with you?*

"Okay," Jason said. "Who's gonna be first?"

I jumped back. His sudden enthusiasm caught me off guard.

Spade hadn't moved. The guy was as tense as a statue.

No one moved. We stood there. Waiting.

Jason smiled. "It's not only simple, it's kind of fun."

With the rifle aimed out the window, Jason squinted. He pressed his open eye to the scope, and aimed. A moment later, he fired off two shots. Sounded like puffs of air slamming into a pillow.

Never heard a gun with a silencer before. Had to admit. Was kind of cool.

Palmeri was at the window. "Headshots. Nice."

"Want a turn?" Jason offered her the rifle.

Palmeri shook her head. "I'm good."

Crystal stepped forward. "I'll give it a shot," she said, and laughed. "No pun intended."

"Ah, but a funny one at that," Jason said, and handed her the rifle. "Here you are, dear."

Crystal aimed and fired. "Huh. Got 'em."

"Nice shooting, nice." Jason clapped.

Crystal took three more shots. "Okay, yeah, this is fun."

There was nothing fun about it. My stomach rolled. Killing the things to survive was one thing, but making a game out of it, a mockery of what we were against, seemed wrong. They had been people.

My ex-wife had been staring at photos of our kids. She was a zombie, but she somehow held onto to some part of her that still possibly felt or thought of being loved.

The others didn't know this. I hadn't found the right time to share some of my suspicions.

"Who's next?" Crystal said, holding the rifle out to anyone.

Charlene took a step.

I grabbed her wrist. Didn't want it obvious to everyone that I was stopping her.

She caught on, stepped back, stood next to me, and stayed still.

Jason took the rifle, offering it to Spade. "How about you? Not much of a challenge for someone of your skill and training, I'm sure. But, just the same, might feel good getting out some of that pent up anger."

"And what makes you think I'm angry?" Spade said.

"In today's world, soldier, who among us isn't angry?"

"Coffee's ready," Jeremy called up to us.

Jason and Spade seemed locked in a staring contest, neither moving a muscle.

Jason gave in first. He aimed it out the window. Five quick shots fired. "Hmm. There we are."

He lowered the rifle and leaned it against the wall.

"Coffee is ready," Jason said. He wove his way between us and left the room.

"We're getting out of here," Spade said. "In the morning. You all get some sleep tonight. I'll keep watch."

"Watch over what?" Sues said. "You heard them. No way can zombies get in here."

Spade sucked in a deep breath. "Isn't zombies I'm worried about tonight."

# CHAPTER TWENTY-EIGHT

I showered before bed. Stood under the spray for as long as I thought allowed. Others wanted in, so I did not want to use all the hot water. Easily could have, but I refrained. The smell of shampoo and Irish Spring soap was in and of itself, invigorating. The dried dirt took serious scrubbing to remove. I had to keep swiping my foot to clear mud from over the tub drain.

After toweling off, I took advantage of the situation, and found an unused razor and shaving cream. Always hated shaving, always. On that night, I reveled in it, enjoying each pass of the blades over my skin. Splashing hot water on my face afterwards, felt both comforting and soothing.

Someone knocked on the door. The moment was chased away.

"Dad, you take longer than me!" Char stepped into the bathroom as I left with a towel wrapped around my waist. "And don't walk around like that. No one wants to see your chest hair, geesh!"

I raised my eyebrows as she closed the door, and went to the bedroom Allison, Charlene and I would share for the night. In the few short steps I took from one door to the next, I'll admit I was fooled.

Caught believing this was normal. Like we were on a vacation. The three of us staying over at some bed and breakfast in the Thousand Islands. In the morning, we'd fish, and walk to town for ice cream.

The illusion didn't immediately vanish. When I walked into the bedroom, Allison was there, smiling.

"Jason brought you a change of clothes. That dress shirt, and vest coat. Gave you a pair of jeans, too," Allison said.

"That was thoughtful."

"Guess, we don't have long. Shut that door, drop that towel and get over here," she said. Demanding. I loved it.

"Good thing, I don't think it will take long," I said. Never one to disobey orders, I did as instructed.

# # #

*Monday, November 2nd -- 0913*

"Rise and shine."

I opened my eyes, expecting either Allison or Charlene to be the one waking me. "Spade?"

"Brothers have been up since dawn. Got bacon on a griddle, scrambling up eggs. Jeremy's making biscuits. They wanted to me to come wake everyone up," he said.

"You get any sleep?" I said.

Allison sat up, while Charlene rolled away from us, pulling blankets over her head.

"Not a wink," he said, and winked. Ironic.

"Hey, man, what's going on here?" I said.

Charlene lowered the blanket and looked at us.

"Oh, they are up. Hurry down or everything will get cold." Jason leaned in the open doorway. "I'll wake the others."

"Just follow my lead," Spade said, in a whisper.

I nodded.

We got out of bed, about to leave the room, when I stopped and strapped on my weapons. Allison and Charlene grabbed their rifles and handguns.

"Wonder if they have holsters. Tucking this Glock in my waistband, not so comfy," Charlene said.

"Stay close, you two," I said.

"What's wrong here," Charlene said.

"I don't know but I feel it. Spade does, too." I took in a breath and sighed. "After we eat, though, I am going to go out back. I am going to bury Cash--"

"I want to help," Charlene said.

"Me, too. We should do it together," Allison said.

I pursed my lips, hoping it resembled a humbled smile. "Okay. That's a good idea. Together."

We walked out of the room. The aroma wafting up from the kitchen was immediate. "Bacon," Charlene said.

"Poor Erway," Allison said.

"I'll eat the eggs, I guess." Erway startled us.

I spun around. "Scared me."

"Sorry about that. How'd you guys sleep?"

"Well," Allison said.

"And that's everyone." Jason closed bedroom doors as he passed them.

"Good morning, everyone." Crystal scratched at a mop of hair. "Where's Elysia?"

"Palmeri?" Erway said. "She went down earlier. She did not sleep well. Tossed and turned all night."

"Didn't bother me," Crystal said.

"Kept me up," Erway said.

We went down the stairs. Our Bed & Breakfast had a home cooked meal waiting, and I'd just bet a day full of activities!

I needed to keep my head on straight. Couldn't allow myself to be sucked into this Never Never Land the Terrigino brothers created.

We took the same seats around the large table. Erway joined us, fitting in on a folding chair at a corner by where Jason sat. The spread took up a lot of the center of the table. There were even two jugs of orange juice, and one of milk. Two oil lamps burned at either end. Gave the whole room a rather relaxing ambiance.

Never Never Land was damned appealing. No doubt about it.

"So," Jason said as he reached for a piece of crisp bacon. "What are your plans?"

The question was vague, and was not seemingly directed at anyone in particular. "I would like permission to borrow shovels so I can bury my son," I said.

No one moved.

"Of course," Jason said. "If you would like, we have a tree out back. Provides lots of shade in the summer months. It's tall, strong. You are more than welcome to use the ground around it, if you'd like."

"That sounds wonderful. Thank you, I appreciate it," I said.

He smiled. "Of course. And Jeremy and I would like some volunteers."

Spade cocked his head to one side. "Volunteers?"

"Need a small hunting party. Dinner doesn't grow on trees. However," he held up a finger, "it can often be found running along the branches."

I heard Jeremy laugh from the kitchen. The door swung open. "Biscuits are just out of the oven. Hot, hot, hot. You can cut 'em open and lay a slab of butter in there. It should melt without spreading it. In my opinion, they are so good that they don't even require butter, but that's just me."

The biscuits looked and smelled amazing.

My plate contained fluffy scrambled eggs, strips of bacon and toast. I could not pass on the biscuits though. Figured, we might not be here long, so I might as well fill my belly. Could be a while before we eat like this again, if ever.

With a glance around the table, it seemed like I wasn't the only one thinking this way, with the exception of the Terrigino brothers. They didn't pile food onto their plates. They knew where the next meal was coming from. It was right in the fridge in the next room.

"I'd be happy to give you a hand, replenishing the food we've eaten," Spade said.

"Thank you," Jason said. "Someone like you, I doubt it would take very long. Jeremy will accompany you."

"I'm pretty sure it's something I can do on my own. We owe you that much. I'm sure your brother has more important things to do if I handle the hunting."

"Like what?" Jason said. It was the first time I'd seen him snap, losing his cool host-like composure.

"I'm sorry?" Spade said. It wasn't an apology, as much as a *who-the-fuck-do-you-think-you're-talking-to* implication.

"No, I'm sorry." Jason forked his eggs around on his plate before lifting a mouthful and taking a bite. He chewed slowly, his eyes never leaving Spade. "I just meant, like what is it you think there is for my brother to do? We're up in the mountains, in the woods, while the world below us is suffering a worse hemorrhage than the black plague."

Spade pushed back from the table. "I saw stacks of wood. Might need more chopped? Winters must be brutal up here."

Using the tip of his tongue to pick at food in the front of his teeth, Jason again smiled, or tried to. "That is excellent. We do spend a lot of time chopping wood. The supply dwindles faster than one might think. We have a pretty efficient wood burning stove, but you are correct. Chopping wood is a daily chore. I *am* sorry if I sounded . . . rude. It's just this, everything going on, it gets to me."

"We've spent nearly a month watching the military prepare that camp down there. Setting up tents and cleaning the apartments inside. They made repairs to the fence, and were always coming and going. Those loud vehicles of theirs. No respect for nature, really," Jeremy said. "We had no clue what was going on. We kept our distance, but never stopped watching them."

"And what did you discover?"

Jason shrugged. "Only that they were expecting to lock a lot of people up inside the razor-wire compound. Of course, we didn't know why, or what the military was preparing for. All the shit going on in nearly every third-world country, and some not-so-third-world, figured a war was coming. We didn't take it lightly, Jeremy and me. We chopped our wood, stocked our freezers, and made sure we had a solid stack of supplies. And then we saw them. . ."

"Them?" Palmeri said.

"Those things. The zombies. They brought a few in strapped to gurneys, flown in on that helicopter of theirs."

"Helicopter?" I said.

"Over by their little landing strip," Jason said, pointing to nowhere in particular. "We thought for sure a new plague hit. That all these infected people were going to be quarantined in our hills. Our hills. That wasn't going to work. Our father, he'd never have stood for it. The American military just moving in with diseased people, destroying our home."

I put a hand on my stomach. Wasn't sure I was going to like the rest of the story.

"What did you do? What did you and your brother do?" Spade said.

"We did nothing. We watched them. We watched the sick they brought in. Had them in collars and kept them tied to posts like dogs. Jeremy said they looked like zombies," he said.

"I did. I knew it," Jeremy said.

"He knew it alright. Then, a few days ago, some of those . . . zombies were outside the fence. Don't think they were the same ones the military delivered to the camp," Jason said.

"I was sure it was Mr. Robinson, guy who ran the little grocery store along the main road," Jeremy said. "And then there was Loretta Breeze, she was in her night gown and just growling and moaning and wandering around aimlessly."

"Military shot them. Put bullets into their heads. Just, killed them. You don't shoot sick people," Jason said.

"And again, I said, they're zombies. Like in the movies."

"More came out of the woods. Started sniffing their way around here. We were left with no choice. We had to shoot them. If the military was that out of sorts to the point they were shooting 'em, it only made sense we should shoot them, too."

"It's the military, or I guess, the government's fault. They brought those things up here," Jeremy said, as he used a knife to slice open a biscuit. "So all we did was cut a hole in their fence. Gave some of the local dead a chance to enter the compound. That's all. Served them right. That's how we see it."

Spade shook his head. "That's how you see it?"

"You see it differently, soldier?" Jason tipped his head to one side. It was confrontational.

"That camp was a mobile research facility. They were going to be studying the creatures, trying to find a cure. They were looking for a way to fix the mess," Spade said.

"A mess they caused," Jason said.

"Dammit, you had no right. Do you know how many people were in there? How many you killed?"

"We didn't kill a single one of them."

"No, but you wanted them gone. Away from your precious land."

"That so wrong? We built this land. This has been with our family for generations, soldier. Generations. It is ours. My brothers and mine. Military has no right infecting the area with their mistakes. None!" Jason slammed a first on the table. Silverware rattled.

"Our father would have done the same," Jeremy said. "We just did what he would have done."

"Then your father was crazy like his boys. Is that what you're telling me?"

Jeremy jumped to his feet. "You take that back, right now. Take it back!"

Spade shook his head. "Not a fucking chance. I had brothers inside that camp, my family. They're all dead because of the stupidity of the two of you. Did you ever think to just go and talk with someone at the camp? Ask a few questions before sabotaging their safety?"

"You think we could just stroll up there and introduce ourselves and ask questions, and they'd be all like, come on in, have some coffee and cookies and we'll give you all the answers you want?" Jason said. "You're a soldier, yes. But you're not a robot, are you? You ever know your military to be upfront and honest about anything?"

"Would have been worth a try, first," Palmeri said.

"A try? A try? I know the soldiers there did a survey of the area. I don't think they knew we lived so close. They never came around to talk to the neighbors, let me tell you. Not once. So either they knew we were there and didn't care to introduce themselves, or they didn't know. I wasn't going to risk what might happen if they found us."

"So you killed them all," Spade said.

Now Jason got to his feet. "We didn't kill any of them!"

"We're leaving," Spade said.

I wanted to bury my son. I took Allison's hand, giving it a quick squeeze. Things were not going well. We were all on alert. I know I was. I wanted to be sure everyone else was, too.

"Leaving? Going where? You're in the middle of nowhere, soldier. This place, our home, it's your best chance to last through the winter. We've got everything you could want. Leaving would be foolish. An argument, no, a simple disagreement and you're just going to up and leave? That's ridiculous," Jason said, and sat back down. He motioned for Jeremy to do the same.

"I still want an apology for what you said about our father," Jeremy said.

"Well, you're not getting one, fuckface," Spade said.

"Name calling, really? Is that what we're resorting to, name calling?" Jason said. "Jeremy, sit down. We need to work past this. Everyone is tense. It's okay. It's expected."

"On behalf of my friends and I, thank you for your hospitality, but after I fetch you some squirrels, and chop a little extra wood for you, we're leaving." Spade kept both hands on the table. The fingers of both hands. Reminded me of the way a gunslinger stood, hands by the gun handles, ready to draw if necessary.

"You want to leave, really? It's so bad is it? A few things, then," Jason said. "Everyone should tell me for themselves whether they want to stay or not. I know you think this is the army, but here, I don't think you call all the shots. I think--"

"You want to ask each one of them, you go right ahead," Spade said. "Ask."

Jason looked around the table. "You all have eaten two wonderful meals, thanks to Jeremy. Thank you, Jeremy."

"Welcome."

"You all slept in warm beds in nice rooms and in a safe log cabin. No reason any of that will ever change. Ever. We work together, we unite as a family, and this little log cabin in the mountains is as good a fortress as the White House -- which, by the way, I hear did not fare well during this apocalypse. So I ask you, each of you, who would like to stay?"

I had to look around. I needed to see expressions on faces.

Dave and Sues both shook their heads. No.

Erway and Palmeri said no, too.

Allison, Charlene and I said no.

Crystal looked undecided.

"Ms. Sutton?" Jason said.

"I'm not sure," she said.

I wanted to lash out, call her a traitor, but was she? The Terrigino's made me nervous, apprehensive. They were crazy, no doubt. Weren't we *all* a little crazy at this point?

Jason nodded. "So, soldier, not everyone wants to leave."

Spade just looked down, clearly disappointed with Crystal. "We're leaving, all of us."

"Except Ms. Sutton," Jason said.

"No. Including Ms. Sutton," Spade said.

# CHAPTER TWENTY-NINE

I didn't want to use the spot by the tree that Jason suggested, out of spite, or principle. However, he'd been right. It was an ideal location. Peaceful. So it was where we dug, but on the opposite side of the tree, not facing the log cabin.

With our weapons against the tree, we took turns shoveling dirt. The ground was cold and hard. All the rain that had fallen had made the ground rock hard now. Chipping away with a pickaxe helped. The work was laborious, but no one complained.

Cash was wrapped in a tarp, just feet away from where we dug. After each shovelful, I couldn't help but look at him. The idea of putting my son into the earth was haunting. Nightmares would plague my sleep forever.

Burying a child was something no one should ever have to do. My heart was broken. Shattered.

We'd cleared roughly four feet in a couple of hours. Despite gardening gloves, my palms were blistered and raw.

Charlene and I gently lifted Cash. She held his legs and I had the shoulders. We placed him into the hole, stood around it, and stared in.

Allison held my hand and laid her head on my chest.

We were all crying and sniffing.

It was time to say something, but I had no words. My emotions ran rampant inside me. I wasn't sure I could speak, or if whatever I chose to say would even be coherent, or make sense. "I'm going to miss you, little buddy. I miss you."

Charlene sobbed, her shoulders shaking. I pulled her in tightly and held her close.

"When you were born," I said. "I brought your sister in to meet you. You were just a tiny thing in your mom's arms. We didn't want your sister to be jealous. Your mom bought a couple of Barbie dolls and had them in her hospital bag. So, when Charlene and I came in to say hello, your mom gave Char the dolls, and said, 'Your brother got these for you.' Charlene took those dolls, and just looked at you like you were the greatest kid in the world and she said. . . Do you remember what you said, Char?"

She ran a sleeve under her nose. "I looked at him and I said, 'Thank you, brother.'"

"Yep, that's what you said. I'll never forget that," I said.

"What are we going to do without him, Daddy?" Charlene knelt by the grave. "I don't want to just leave him here. Out here. All alone."

"I don't either."

We were silent while we filled the dirt back into the hole. I tried my best not to think about what it was we were actually doing. As we patted down the earth, I saw Spade and Jeremy approach the side of the log cabin.

Dave and the others had spent a better part of the morning loading the zombies killed from the bedroom window last night onto a wheelbarrow and moving them far off the Terrigino property. To where, I hadn't a clue.

"Listen, I have a bad feeling about how things are going to go down. I want both of you ready and on alert at all times. Got it?" I said.

They nodded. We grabbed up our weapons and carried the shovels back to the cabin.

Jason was out on the front porch smoking a cigarette.

I didn't know he had those. I wanted one. A pack. A carton. I'd settle for one.

"It's nearly four. We all worked through lunch so we'll have an early dinner. I've got mashed potatoes. They're from a box, but with enough butter and salt, you'll never know the difference," Jason said.

"Thank you, but no thank you," Spade said.

"Still have your heart set on leaving?"

An early dinner did sound good. It would be dark soon, I thought. Almost had to shake my head to clear away the thoughts.

"We are. We'll just make sure we have our things and we'll be going."

Erway, Palmeri, and Crystal came out of the cabin.

I didn't see Dave or Sues. I checked the woods, but saw nothing.

"Okay, but I must tell you. In order for you to leave, there are two things you need to know." Jason smiled.

I hated that smile.

Spade took an aggressive stance. "Yeah? And what's that?"

"The weapons. They're ours, not yours, so you can't have them. We'll be wanting those back," he said.

All I could think was, *oh shit!*

Spade snickered, as if he thought Jason was telling a joke. "And the other thing?"

"Aside from Crystal staying with us, so are the other women."

"W-what?" That last comment even caught Spade off guard.

"It's the end of the world. It has to restart somehow, by someone. Better people like us--survivalists, than the likes of you. The women, they're staying."

"My daughter's fourteen," I said, as if it mattered, like there was any chance in hell I'd leave my kid here.

Spade took a step toward Jason. I saw it before it happened and was helpless to do anything.

Jeremy raised his gun and shot Spade in the back of the head. Spade fell forward in a heap with arms splayed out, blood and brain spilling from the cracked bowl that was his shattered skull.

"No!" I yelled. "Are you out of your fucking--"

I spread my arms wide, pushing Allison and Charlene behind me as Jeremy pointed his gun at me.

Jeremy's chest exploded like his heart ruptured. He dropped his gun and clapped both hands over his heart, falling to his knees.

I hadn't heard a shot. I didn't know what had just--

The upstairs window.

The barrel of a rifle protruded.

Jason was screaming and he started to run for his brother. Palmeri reached for him, tugged on his sleeve. It probably saved his live. Another shot sent a chunk of dirt and crisp leaves into the air. Looking up, Jason now knew where Dave and Sues were.

Like a cheetah, he spun around and ran for the house.

Erway tried to stop him. He pushed her aside, pulled his gun, fired as he ran into the house, and slammed the front door.

"He's inside," I said, looking up at the window. "He's in the house!"

"Crystal's been shot," Palmeri said. She knelt beside the woman.

"How's it look," Allison said, running over to them.

I was at the front door, throwing my shoulder into it. Steel. As Jason promised, there was no way to knock it open. At the window, with the shutters open for the day, I used the shovel like a baseball bat and smashed the glass.

"The shot's to the stomach," Erway said. She had blood dripping from her lip, and nose. She tore a piece of Crystal's shirt at the bullet hole, exposing the gut wound. The blood bubbled and pooled on her belly. With a gentle swipe of her hand, Erway cleared most of the blood off.

I used the shovel blade as if I was ringing a triangle, and knocked all the shards of loose and protruding glass from the frame before I climbed in through the bay window headfirst. Jason saw and fired at me.

Heat burned my skin on my right shoulder. I fell back out. "Dave, he's in the house!"

"Daddy!" Charlene left Allison's side and ran to mine. She looked at my shoulder. Copying Erway, she dug her fingers into the clothing hole, and pulled the material apart. I tried to look.

"I don't think it went in. A graze," I said. Sure felt like it went in. If a graze hurt like this, as if my skin was on fire, I couldn't imagine what getting shot actually felt like.

Cash had been shot.

"You look okay," she said.

"All this shooting, it's going to be like ringing a dinner bell for the zombies. Keep an eye on everything. Don't let them sneak up on us," I said.

Charlene stood up, held out her hand and pulled me to my feet.

I was more cautious this time, and looked through the open window. I hoisted myself up and into the log cabin. I removed the machete from the sheath over my back. I stood still, listening, my eyes looking everywhere. Jason knew Dave was upstairs. Would he have gone right up after them? Did he think he'd killed me?

The stairs were right in front of me.

The urge to yell out for Dave and Sues was so strong that I almost had to bite my tongue to keep quiet. I took a few small steps toward the staircase. The silence was maddening.

Through the smashed out window, though, I could hear Erway and Palmeri working on Crystal, each one barking out different things.

They needed supplies to save that woman.

I knew where the medical supplies were. In that room with all the weapons.

We needed to stop Jason first. He was the threat. Then we could concentrate on helping Crystal. It was the only thing I could come up with that sounded remotely rational.

I put a foot on the first step.

It squeaked.

The bedroom door, behind which my son died, flew open.

Jason came out of the room holding a lit, oil filled lantern. He flung it across the room. The beveled glass shattered. The oil splashed out onto everything, and fire quickly followed.

The sofa and carpet caught first, then the curtains next.

In that instant, Jason was on me, knocking me back against the wall.

Flames crackled. I heard Charlene outside screaming for me.

Jason punched me in the solar plexus causing air to rush out of my lungs. Gasping, I tried my hardest to fill them with air. The man didn't stop, didn't let up.

His fists were like rocks. It felt like ribs were snapping with each blow delivered.

I knew what the man thought. There was no way he was going to win, kill us all. His plan had failed, and because of it, his brother was dead, so he had nothing to lose at this point. He would destroy the cabin, and go down fighting.

Jeremy would have said, "It's what our father would have wanted."

I closed my eyes and ignored the pain in my chest. I used my head like a fist and broke Jason's nose with my forehead. The crunch of bone was satisfying.

His eyes watered, and he backed a step away from me. It was all the time and room I needed.

I noticed the brass knuckles on his fist, fucking bastard. I stepped into my punch, used all my weight, and drove my elbow into his face. He went down. "Dave!"

I stomped on his back with my foot, then kicked him across his already bloodied face. It knocked him out. "Dave!"

I heard them upstairs.

Dave and Sues were at the top of the stairs. "We were trying to get out the window. We didn't know you were in here."

"Come on, get out. We have to get out!"

They came down the stairs.

Sues jumped over Jason's body. "Dave," she said, as she unlocked and pulled open the front door.

The flames were everywhere. The heat was more intense than I could ever have imagined. I saw orange and black flames roll up across the ceiling, like spilled fluid, except upside down.

Dave pulled on my arm.

"Let's hit the weapons room. We need more," I said.

"Fast," Dave said. He didn't call me crazy or stupid, he just ran toward that room.

Inside, he grabbed for guns and ammo.

I took an armful of sheathed machetes and swords. I grabbed a few hunting knives. I knew these were going to be our weapons on the road. Ammo was always bound to run out. "Let's go. Let's --"

"You're not going anywhere," Jason said. He looked like a monster with his swollen and bruised face. At this point, it was more purple and black than white. He stood right at the door. Smoke began to fill the room. There were no windows in this…closet space. Just weapons and enough ammo to make the entire cabin explode. "None of us are."

Jason had a gun, and he had his finger inside the trigger.

"Let them out of there!" That was Palmeri's voice.

I don't think Jason expected anyone to enter the burning cabin. Bet he thought shooting us would be too lenient, and us burning to death was a far better punishment.

Jason flinched, but didn't turn around.

"Drop the gun, or I'll shoot you in the mother-fucking back, Terrigino," Palmeri said. "You know what? I have no time for this."

Jason dropped his gun.

Palmeri opened fire. Shots into his back propelled through his body and out his chest and stomach. His body jerked and twisted as he fell forward, hitting the table in the center of the room.

Dave and I finished picking up what we needed. Palmeri grabbed a few things, too. Then we ran back through to the main room. Fire ate at the walls. Smoke darkened the room to almost zero visibility.

We were never going to get out.

"Get low," Palmeri said.

Dave and I dropped to our knees. Crawling was nearly impossible with all of the weapons in tow. I did my best to move forward without relinquishing the machetes and swords. It was not easy and moving was slow.

Too slow.

The wood creaked above us. The ceiling was weakening. We needed to get out. Fast.

We were in a row. I was behind Palmeri and Dave was behind me. I just kept my eyes on Palmeri's feet.

At the door, Palmeri escaped, and then I did.

I turned around. My eyes tearing from the smoke and heat. I coughed and coughed, trying to clear my lungs.

"Dave!" I said.

"Right here, brother," he said.

I think I've officially quit smoking. Not just because I didn't have a single cigarette, but also because my lungs felt black as fucking charcoal right now.

"You guys okay?" Allison said.

"Yeah. Yes," I said. My shoulder hurt. "How's Crystal?"

"Ah, dead," Erway said. "But that's not our biggest concern right now."

I pushed up onto an elbow. The fire was consuming the entire cabin. All the food and luxuries. The shampoo and soap. "It's not? Why?"

"Because they are!"

I looked where Erway pointed.

Charlene had one of the machetes I'd retrieved and was running at a small horde of zombies emerging from the woods.

Sues kissed Dave on the forehead, grabbed another machete and ran after my daughter.

I almost yelled for them to stop.

They couldn't stop, because it's what needed to be done. I stood up and broke into a sprint.

Dave and I came upon the zombies a split second after Charlene and Sues engaged them.

The machetes were sharp. In two swift swipes, I sliced off an arm and a head.

With both hands on the handle, Dave raised the blade over his head and brought it down in an arcing swing, cutting through a zombie's skull as if clearing weeds in a jungle.

Charlene took out the legs on a fast zombie. Just dropped low and swung. The thing went down, face first. She came up behind it and chopped at its head three times.

It was kind of like cracking a coconut, just a little easier with these blades...

# CHAPTER THIRTY

We had the clothing on our back, some guns, some machetes, swords and knives, but nothing else. Well, that wasn't true, not exactly. We had each other. It sounded cheesy as all get out, but it was true, so I couldn't deny it.

I had my girls. Allison and Charlene.

Dave was with Sues, and there was Erway and Palmeri.

The seven of us.

"Now what?" Charlene said.

The log cabin burned behind us. We'd ventured into the woods. We hadn't left, just found a place to hide, away from the fire. Zombies might hate water, but they loved fire.

"Those brothers must have a vehicle somewhere," Dave said. "How'd they get back and forth? They didn't hike everywhere, did they?"

"I didn't see any other buildings," Sues said. "No barn, no garage."

"Me either," Dave said.

"In the morning, maybe we should go back to the internment camp and see if there's anything in there we can salvage. Military had vehicles bringing people in and out, so there must be something down there," Palmeri said.

I nodded. "I like it. Makes sense."

"Where are we supposed to sleep?" Charlene said.

"Out here under the stars." Sues looked up at the sky.

"We're going to freeze," she said. "It's not like we can start a fire."

My daughter was right. We couldn't have a fire. We just might freeze. "We're going to need to find shelter somewhere."

I waited for ideas. Any suggestion at all. No one had one. I didn't want to be the one to say it. "We could go back to the camp now and clear one of those apartments."

"You want to go back there now?" Dave said.

I knew he hated that place. I hated it, too. It had been horrible. A dark maze that I felt for sure we were going to die inside of. "You have a better idea?"

He shook his head. "Wish I did, but I don't, though."

"Anyone?"

No one said a word.

We took a moment to get the weapons on in a way we liked. My daughter copied my look exactly. The sword, knife on the hip and machete over the back.

In a line, we walked toward the camp, past the river where the Coast Guard had once been docked and had once seemed like our saviors. Daylight was gone. The mountain and trees were to our west. For us, it seemed the sun had set hours ago.

The fence surrounding the camp was just like how I remembered it, foreboding. The coiled razor wire running along the top just added to the overall eeriness of the situation.

"This is where we were going to stay?" Charlene said.

"Ah, yep."

"Not," she said.

"It's where we're going to stay now," I said.

"There has to be something better," she said.

I would have loved to agree, but I doubted it.

Palmeri had point. We moved a little faster than the first time out to the camp. Palmeri wasn't messing around. She wanted to get us somewhere safe and she wanted it done in a hurry. I was good with that.

We stopped when we reached the closed gate entrance. It was closed, but I looked at the ground. The belt I had secured the fence with was unbuckled. The  belt was on the wet, cold ground. I looked through the links, and shook my head.

"What?" Charlene said.

The zombies we'd killed last time were still dead. That was a little bit of peace of mind that I had no trouble clinging onto, but the belt . . . that was something else altogether. "Nothing," I said.

"We go in?" Allison said.

"Wait," Palmeri said. "We know there's another opening in this fence. Let's just stay outside the chain link for now. Circle around and see exactly what we're dealing with. I'm not all that excited about locking myself in there without knowing where all the openings are."

"Okay, let's walk the outside of the fence," Dave said.

Again, we followed Palmeri.

I kept looking through the fence at the compound, and toward the surrounding woods. Military did pick an excellent, out of the way spot for the camp. It looked like the land had been cleared specifically for the government, which if I thought about that is exactly what they must have done. Cleared it with plans for the camp. Good ol' US of A.

"What's that?" Sues said. I thought she'd spoken a little too loudly. I was many people behind everyone and I heard her as if she'd just whispered in my ear.

Palmeri stopped.

"It's not a parking lot," Sues said. "Is it a parking lot?"

It did in fact look like a parking lot. A sizeable one, at that.

"We're not going to have to dig through dead people's clothing for keys, are we?"

"Won't have to," Palmeri said. "Military vehicles. There are no keys. Can you imagine in the middle of a war -- not too unlike this -- and our troops need to get out and get away fast? You want to all be standing around, everyone patting their pockets looking for who had the keys last?"

That was an excellent point. One I had never thought of.

It just sounded way too good to be true, and when something sounded way too good to be true, it usually was.

We made our way from the fence, across grass and weeds to the parking lot. We all stayed low.

I stood, leaned my back on a Humvee grille and scanned the woods. Moon was out. Sky was clear.

I saw nothing coming at us.

"We're good, so far," I said.

Palmeri opened the Humvee door. I circled around the vehicle. Could not believe how quiet the night was. Were all the zombies at the house fire? Were they inside the encampment?

"Climb in, everyone," Palmeri said.

"Son of a bitch," Dave said. "Can you believe it?"

Everyone had opened a door to the Humvee when I heard it. A moan.

"Dad!"

Palmeri pushed a button, starting the engine. "Get in."

I saw him. A fast shadow.

He came at me, right at me.

I raised my machete, holding it like a baseball player at home plate.

It was Marfione. Marf.

His face had bites ripped out of it, his eyes…milky and lifeless. He was covered in mud and tattered clothing, I could smell him before I could reach him with my blade.

I stepped into the swing. The machete cut with ease. I severed the head and right arm at the shoulder, causing his body to flop onto the loose gravel. "Sorry about that, Marf. I am. I'm sorry about that."

"Get in, Daddy, get in."

Felt a little like deja vu. Palmeri and Erway sat up front.

Dave and Sues sat across from me.

Allison and Charlene sat on either side of me.

Only thing missing was Cash.

"Everything is going to be fine," I said.

And the Academy Award goes to…


THE END…

Don't missing the thrilling conclusion to the VACCINATION
Trilogy in
Phillip Tomasso's
PRESERVATION

**Coming Soon** from SEVERED PRESS

About the Author

Phillip Tomasso is the award winning author of numerous novels, and short stories. He works full time as a Fire/EMS Dispatcher at 911. He lives in Rochester, NY with his three children, dog, Fettuccine and cat, Luca. He is always at work on his next tale.

www.philliptomasso.com / phillip@philliptomasso.com
@P_Tomasso

Other Titles by Tomasso

Vaccination
Sounds of Silence
Pulse of Evil
Pigeon Drop
Convicted
The Molech Prophecy (as Thomas Phillips)
Adverse Impact
Johnny Blade
Third Ring
Tenth House
Mind Play